the trouble with

♥ flying

Also by Rachel Morgan

RACHEL MORGAN

the trouble with

flying

THE TROUBLE WITH FLYING

Copyright © 2014 Rachel Morgan

ISBN 978-0-9922339-3-8

RACHEL
MORGAN

For all the shy people

1

I DON'T MAKE FRIENDS ON AEROPLANES. I KNOW THERE are people who like to strike up a conversation with the complete stranger sitting next to them, but that's not me. It's not that I'm an unfriendly person. It's more the fact that the conversation centre of my brain seems to seize up in the presence of strangers, and I can't for the life of me figure out what to say. And even if the other person is happy to simply babble on while I pretend to be interested, I'd rather be doing something else. Like reading. Or watching a movie. Or trying to figure out how to stop crying.

Yes. Crying. Because if being shy and awkward isn't enough, today I'm adding red eyes, tears, and suppressed sobs to the embarrassing mix.

I stare out the oval window at the patches of reflected light on the wet runway and silently ask God to leave the seat next to me empty. I can't deal with a chatty neighbour right now. I'd rather watch the black sky and incessant rain until we reach cruising altitude. Then I'll close my eyes and let sleep take the pain away.

Oh, STOP IT. It's not like someone died.

I wiggle around a bit in my seat and sniff, trying to listen to my inner pep-talk voice. *Think of the good things*, I tell myself. I'm on my way home. I'm leaving behind the dreary, wet weather for a sunny, summer climate. That, at least, should make me happy. But thinking about home leads to thoughts of *who* I'm flying towards, and that only makes my stomach twist further.

I hear the sound of a bag being dumped onto the seat at the end of my row. There are only three seats between the window and the aisle—mine and two others—so there's a fifty-fifty chance this person is about to plonk him or herself down right next to me.

I angle myself towards the window and swipe my fingers beneath my eyes. I start the furious tear-banishing blinking. *Stop crying, stop crying, stop crying.* All I need now is for someone to see my blotchy, wet face and start asking me what's wrong.

Someone settles into a seat. I don't feel movement right beside me, though, so it must be the aisle seat. Fantastic. I send up a quick thank-you prayer and remind God that it would be spectacularly awesome if He could keep the seat next to me empty.

A tickle inside my left nostril alerts me to the fact that my nose is dribbling. I sniff, but it doesn't help. *Crap, where are my tissues?* I lean forward and reach down by my feet for my handbag. Brown strands of hair fall in front of my face and block my vision, but if I can just get the zip open and feel past my purse to the tissues—

No. Too late. Now it's trickling down my lip and I'm digging around in the bag and I can't feel the stupid tissues and a drop of tear snot just landed on my hand and *yuck*! I haul the ridiculous handbag—I told Jules I didn't need something so big—onto my lap with one hand while holding the back of my other hand to my nose. And there the tissues are. Right next to my purse. Practically mocking me. I rip one from the packet and jam it against my nose to stop the tear-snot flood.

And that's when I catch a glimpse of the guy sitting in the aisle seat. A quick sideways glimpse, but enough to tell me he's cute. Excellent cheekbones, a strong jawline, and perfectly messy dark brown hair. Terrific. My nose is dripping snot in front of a cute guy. Not that I should care that he's cute, or that he's a guy, because it's not like I'm going to talk to him, and it's not like I'm even available—am I? I don't actually know. And thinking about *that* makes me want to cry all over again—but STILL. I don't want to look blotchy and snotty in front of a cute guy.

I turn back to the window because I'm going to have to blow my nose now, and I *hate* doing that in front of other people. Such revolting noises. I take a deep breath and go for it, cringing at how loud it sounds. I grab another tissue and finish cleaning up my face, then find an empty side pocket on my handbag to stuff the wadded tissues into. *Gross.* I wish I'd stocked up on waterless hand sanitiser after

I finished my last bottle.

I drop my handbag onto the floor and straighten. From the corner of my eye, I take a peek at the cute guy, half expecting to find him giving me a disgusted look. I needn't have worried. He's holding the two halves of the seatbelt in his hands and staring at them as if he's never seen a contraption like it before. He pushes the two metal pieces together, and a satisfied half-smile appears on his face when the buckle remains fastened. Weird. Perhaps this guy is a little ... slow. Hopefully that means he won't be interested in chatting.

More passengers squeeze along the aisles; tired parents try to get overexcited children to sit down; businessmen remove their laptops before sliding their bags into the overhead storage compartments. I pull my book from the seat pocket in front of me. I put it there as soon as I found my seat earlier so I'd be ready to act as if I'm reading the moment someone sits down next to me. I open up to the last page I read and try to focus on the story—a sweet, predictable romance meant to distract me from my own messy love life—but the cute guy in the aisle seat keeps shifting around, and I can't help wondering what's wrong with him.

I take another peek. He certainly doesn't look comfortable. Wiggling, tapping his fingers on the armrests, his knees bouncing up and down.

"It's my first time," he says, looking over at me before I can look away. "In a plane, I mean. Never flown anywhere before. So, yeah. A little nervous."

"Your first time flying?" I repeat. I've just broken my own rule—don't perpetuate conversation with strangers if you can help it—but I'm so surprised he's never flown anywhere before that I guess the words just popped out.

"Yeah. Strange, I know. Twenty-three years on this planet and I've never left the ground. Well, there was that giant swing at Adrenalin Quarry—" his fingers drum the armrests repeatedly "—but I guess that doesn't count since the swing itself was still attached to the ground. Certainly felt like flying, though, and flying isn't something I've ever been keen on doing."

He takes a deep breath while I try to figure out if I should tell him that flying in a plane doesn't really feel like *actual flying*—not the way whooshing through the air on a high swing feels—or if I should make an excuse to get back to the safety of my book.

"I'm sorry, I don't usually ramble on like this," he continues. "Must be the nerves. I'm still not entirely convinced this giant metal contraption is going to stay up in the air." He lets out a nervous laugh.

I need to pick up my book and put some headphones on before I say something monumentally stupid. Like last week on the Tube when the foreign guy sitting next to me asked, 'Is that the new Stephen King?' I showed him the bright pink cover of my book and said, 'No, it's a Melissa Carly novel. She's a romance writer,' and wondered where on earth he'd got the idea it might be by Stephen King. How was I supposed to know the guy was *actually* referring to a flier on the seat beside me advertising an album by some rock star named Stevie Keene?

So embarrassing.

Anyway, not only is First-Time-Flying Guy cute, but he has the kind of British accent that makes me feel all swoony. And swoony feelings only aid in sending my conversation skills into freeze mode. So I find it rather surprising when my mouth opens and coherent words come out of it: "There must have been a really good reason for you to get on this plane, then."

"Family reunion," he says. "I was forced."

I smile in response. It would probably be polite of me to ask him something about his family reunion. Something like ... like ... Okay, conversation centre is shutting down. And it's not like *he* asked *me* a question, so I don't have to respond, do I? I can safely return to my book. I look down at my lap, then think of one thing I could say. One thing I *should* say, even though I don't want to. I look over at him. "Um, since it's your first time flying, do you want to sit by the window?"

"No!" he says a little too quickly. "I mean, no, thank you. I'm fine right here. I, um, don't need to see how high we'll be going."

"Oh, it's really not so bad. Once we get up there, we'll be so high you can't even see the ground properly."

He blinks. He stares at me with gorgeous blue-green eyes that say, *You are so not helping.*

"And, um, it's night time anyway, so you won't be able to see the ground at all. Just the lights."

More staring.

Crap. I'm so bad at this.

With my face burning, I look down, pretending to be fascinated by a small hole in the fabric of my seat. I think I can pretty much guarantee First-Time-Flying Guy won't be speaking to me again. I run my finger over the hole, then shake my head and turn back to my book. I find my place on the page and try to get back into the story. The main character has finally realised she's in love with the guy she grew up next door to, but she's convinced, of course, that he'll only ever see her as a friend. She's in the process of planning a makeover for herself in the hopes of getting him to notice her. I'm predicting it'll somehow backfire.

Despite the fact that it's hardly an award-winning novel, I find myself sucked into the cheesy story. The rumbling of the plane's engine helps to lull me into that faraway book world I lose myself in so often, and I'm barely aware of the overhead compartments slamming shut and the flight attendants doing their seatbelt and in-case-of-emergency demonstrations. I'm pulled back to the present when, with a small lurch, the plane begins moving.

"Please say something," First-Time-Flying Guy blurts out.

Startled, the only word that pops out of my mouth is "What?" I lower my book and look at him, but he's staring straight ahead, his fingers tapping a speedy rhythm on the armrests.

"Talk. Anything. Distract me."

"Um ..." *Talk?* Seriously? He might as well ask me to fly the plane myself.

At that moment, I become aware of the fact that the seat right next to me is empty. And since the plane is about to take off, I'm guessing it's going to stay that way for this flight. THANK YOU! Except … now there's no buffer between me and the guy who seems intent on making me talk. Hmm. I really need to be more specific with my prayers.

"I need a distraction," he says, his eyes pleading with mine. "From the flying thing. I know it's irrational. Completely irrational. I mean, I'm a scientist. I trust science. And flying an aeroplane is based on science. But being *in* one … in the sky …" He shakes his head. "I know it's a stupid fear. I know I'm more likely to die in a car accident. But no matter how many times I try to convince myself that flying is perfectly safe these days, my stupid brain keeps reminding me that every now and then things *do* go wrong. And people *do* die. And that this could very well be my moment. To die."

Sheesh. I thought my brain was messed up for being unable to form intelligible sentences in front of strangers, but at least my brain doesn't keep telling me I'm going to *die*.

The silence stretches out between us like soft toffee. "I'm sorry," he says eventually. "Did I scare you? Are you also afraid of flying?"

I shake my head. *Don't. Freak. Out. Just talk!* "No, I'm fine. Flying's not too bad. Really. The worst part is taking off. Or maybe landing. But everything in between is fine. I promise."

Yes! I spoke more than ten words without stumbling over

any of them, and this time I may have actually helped this guy instead of freaking him out further.

"Whoa, okay, we're speeding up." His hands stop their tapping and squeeze the armrests.

Right, so maybe I didn't help *that* much.

"So I'm expecting my ears to start hurting when we take off," he continues, "because of the changing pressure. My sister told me to chew gum, and I know I definitely packed some, but of course I left it in my bag up there, so I guess it's too late for that." He forces his head back against the headrest and closes his eyes. "You idiot, just *shut up*."

I can't help smiling. I think he's forgotten he's talking out loud. "Where are you going?" I ask, raising my voice as the rumbling beneath us grows louder. "I mean, on the other side of Dubai. Obviously we're all going there first, or we wouldn't be on this plane."

He opens his eyes and twists his head to look at me. "What makes you think I'm not staying in Dubai? Maybe I have a wife and two children there."

My ears start to heat up. *You see?* I tell myself. *This is why you should keep quiet.*

"I'm kidding," he says. "South Africa. Half my family lives there, which is why I'm being forced to cross continents for this reunion thing." His eyes slide past me to the window as the vibration beneath our feet increases and our seats start to rattle. "And as much as I appreciate you trying to distract me, I'm fully aware of the fact that we are going way, *way* too fast right now and—oh bloody heck we're in the air!" The plane tilts back as the wheels leave the ground and we begin our ascent. First-Time-Flying Guy presses his head back against the seat once more and squeezes his eyes shut. "Please don't explode, please don't explode, please don't explode."

"It's not going to explode!" I say.

Pain begins to build inside my ears along with the stuffed-with-cotton-wool feeling. I open my mouth and move my jaw around, causing my ears to pop. No chewing gum for me. I've never liked the texture. Makes me feel like I'm eating a super squishy toy.

"Oh dear God, I can see the lights. They're getting smaller." His eyes are glued to my window, despite the fact that he said he didn't want to know how high we'd be going. "Is it supposed to rattle this much? And *bugger*, my ears are hurting."

"Make yourself yawn," I tell him.

"What? I can't *make* myself yawn."

"Yes you can. Or move your jaw around. With your mouth open."

Frowning, he obeys my instruction. Then he winds up yawning for real. And then his eyes slide back to the window, and the panicked expression is on his face once more.

I twist in my seat so I'm facing him and try to cover the window with my back. "South Africa," I say loudly. "I'm going there too. That's where I'm from. I was in England on holiday. Visiting my older sister. She moved there two years ago. She's awesome. Really fun. She makes me laugh all the time."

Oh my goodness, can you pick something just a little *less random to talk about? And maybe try sounding less like a robot reciting facts?*

"That's … cool," First-Time-Flying Guy says.

"And … um … so, I'm really looking forward to feeling the sun on my skin again. I've been wrapped up like a burrito for way too long. I mean, how do you guys survive the entirety of winter? Three weeks was enough for me. I don't know how I'd survive any more of this rain and wind and paralyzing iciness."

Wow. Are you really talking about the weather?

He takes a deep breath and lets it out slowly as the plane starts to feel more horizontal. No more rattling. Just flying. Smooth flying. He peers over my shoulder once more, then leans back in his seat. "Okay," he says quietly, probably to himself. "We're in the air. I can do this."

"Yes, you can," I say, then feel like slapping myself. He wasn't asking for my opinion. He wasn't even talking to me anymore.

"So … I should probably apologise," he adds. I look up, but his eyes refuse to meet mine.

"What? Why?" I can't remember him doing anything wrong.

"For that whole … panicking thing. We haven't exploded yet, so I'm starting to realise my over-the-top reaction wasn't exactly necessary. And I can't really remember what I said to you while it was happening, so I hope it wasn't too embarrassing."

I shake my head. "Don't worry, it wasn't. Not as embarrassing as my weather rambling."

"Oh really?" He raises both eyebrows. "I must have missed that while I was contemplating the plane making a nosedive towards the ground."

"Well, now that I know what was actually going through your mind, I kinda wish you *were* listening to my silly rambling."

Oh my fuzzy beanie. I'm having a conversation. A normal conversation. With someone I don't know. I look down at the closed book in my lap as I try to hide the idiotic smile stretching my lips.

"What?" he asks. I guess I didn't hide it very well.

"I just … don't normally do this." Whoa, okay, I think that's where I was supposed to say, 'Nothing.'

"Do what?" he asks. "Talk about the weather?"

It's officially blurt-it-all-out time. "Talk to strangers."

"Of course," he says, keeping a straight face. "Because talking to strangers is the height of dangerous. At least, that's what our mothers always told us."

"What I *mean*," I say, "is that I *can't* talk to strangers. I freak out. My mind goes blank and I don't know what to say."

"Ah, so that's why you looked so scared earlier when I asked you to talk to me."

"Well, honestly, yes." A hint of heat warms my cheeks again. "Talking to people I don't know is one of my Big Fears in Life."

"You don't seem to be having a problem right now."

Except for the blushing part, which I never seem to be able to control. "I guess you don't really count as a stranger anymore, since I managed to talk you through a near panic attack just now." *And it probably helped that you freaked out in the first place instead of acting cool and confident,* I add silently.

"Yes. There was the near panic attack. But you don't even know my name, so in that regard I'm still a stranger."

"True." I stare at him, waiting.

He holds his hand out. "I'm Aiden."

I wipe my hand quickly against my jeans—in case of clamminess—and grasp his. It's warm, and his handshake is firm. "Sarah," I tell him.

"There," he says. "Now I definitely don't count as a stranger anymore."

THE TEAR-SNOT HAND. HE'S SHAKING THE TEAR-SNOT hand. I cringe inside but manage to stop myself from snatching my hand away. I let go of him and wrap my fingers around my book. My safety blanket. I smile at Aiden—and my mind goes blank again.

Dammit!

I look down and fumble to open the pages of my book. Where was I? I was on page ... page ...

"Don't you use a bookmark?" Aiden asks.

I stop my fumbling and raise my eyes to his. He starts laughing. It's an easy, comfortable sound. He must have forgotten he's inside a flying metal tube. "What?" I ask.

"Your face," he says. "I can tell exactly what you're thinking."

I close the book and cross my arms. "And what exactly am I thinking?"

His laughter gives way to a grin. "'Why is he still talking to me?'"

I open my mouth, but no words come out. Yes, that's pretty much what I was thinking.

"I'm sorry," he says, "but I'm viewing this as something of a challenge. You can't tell me that you never have conversations with strangers and *not* expect me to try and keep you talking for the whole flight."

I raise my eyebrows. Did he say *whole flight?* Because that is definitely not happening.

"So tell me, Sarah. Why are you so afraid of talking to new people?"

"Why are you so afraid of flying?" I ask, finding my voice.

He hesitates for a beat, the smile lines disappearing from around his eyes, then says, "I have a paralysing fear of heights."

"Well, clearly I have a paralysing fear of new people."

"Why?" he asks, looking as though he'd genuinely like to know the answer.

"What is this, a therapy session?" I demand. "*I don't know why!* I guess that's just the way God made me." Why am I shouting? What is *wrong* with me?

"Well, if I were you, and if God were real, I'd ask him what he was thinking."

"God *is* real, and perhaps He made me this way so that I wouldn't annoy strangers who don't want to hear what I have to say."

He pretends to look wounded. "You don't want to hear

what I have to say?"

"No." I wave my book in his face. "I'd rather find out what happens to Jacinda and Max." Wrong. I'd rather listen to Aiden's delicious accent for the next several hours. But the thought of having to engage intelligently is too terrifying for me to indulge in that fantasy.

"That frivolous stuff?" He gestures to the hot pink cover of my book. "You've probably predicted the entire storyline already."

"That's not the point. I still like to read to the end to make sure I'm right. And to answer your question, no. I don't use bookmarks. I remember the last page I was on."

"That seems like a waste of brain space."

"Maybe for you. I, on the other hand, have plenty of brain space."

He watches me, and I get the feeling he's trying not to laugh. He looks at his watch. "Ten minutes in," he says. "You're doing well. Only six hours and thirty-five minutes left."

"No." I hold up a hand. "That's not happening."

"It's already happening, Sarah." He takes the book off my lap and stuffs it into the pocket in front of him.

"Give that back." My heart starts pounding at double speed. I reach across the empty seat to retrieve my safety blanket.

"Sarah, please." He touches my arm, and as the floor shudders slightly beneath our feet, I see the uneasiness in his eyes. He isn't making me talk simply to force me out of my comfort zone. He's making me talk to distract himself from the flight.

I realise I'm being ridiculous. After one last glance at the book I don't really want to read anyway, I pull my arm back slowly. I can do this. After all, Aiden already knows about my stupid fear, so if I blank in the middle of a conversation, he won't think any worse of me than he already does.

"Okay," I say slowly. "Um ..." *Don't be weird, don't be weird, just be normal.*

From the corner of my eye, I see the Fasten Seatbelt light blink off. Before I know it, I'm unclipping the straps across my lap. "I need to go to the toilet," I blurt out, even though I went just before we boarded.

"Really? You need to go *right now?*" Aiden doesn't move his legs. "We just took off."

"Do you want me to pee on the seat?" I demand.

He narrows his eyes. "You don't need to pee."

"Fine, if you won't let me past, then I'll have to climb over you." I raise my leg, but he moves both of his aside before I'm forced to embarrass myself by straddling him.

"You know you can't hide in the bathroom for the entire flight, right?" he says loudly enough for the passengers across the aisle to give us an odd look.

I hurry away from him in the direction of the nearest toilet.

"Don't be long," he calls after me. "You have about three minutes before I have another panic attack."

"Liar," I mutter. The panic attack was probably fake. He's probably been on a plane a hundred times before and this is his way of getting unsuspecting girls to fawn all over him.

I pull open the door of the first toilet I reach and squeeze myself into the tiny space. I shut the door and take a deep breath as I lean against it. "Don't be weird, don't be weird, just be normal," I quietly instruct myself.

This isn't the first time I've locked myself into a small room to give myself a few moments to remember that new people *aren't* actually that scary and that I need to stop being so ridiculously shy. There was the day I started high school, and the day I started university, and the night before my first date with Matt …

Okay. Now is *not* the time to be thinking about Matt.

I push myself away from the door and stare at the mirror. Yuck. Aeroplane bathrooms officially have the worst lighting ever. Even a supermodel would feel ugly in here. I rub my hands over my face before leaning a little closer to my reflection. It could be the horrific lighting in here, but the brown eyes that peer back at me look a little red-rimmed. I guess I shed a lot more tears earlier than I planned to. My hair is flat, the glowing tan I worked so hard on before leaving South Africa has faded, and I've got no makeup on. Bottom line? Even if Aiden was a freak who faked panic attacks to pick up girls on aeroplanes—which I'm pretty sure he's not—he'd have no reason to choose me.

Still, I'm the one he was unfortunate enough to sit next to, so if he needs me to distract him from the chasm of space between us and the ground, I'll do it. It'll be good for me.

I push back the sleeves of my hoodie—green with the words BOOK FREAK across the front—and wash my hands. After drying them, I try to fluff my hair up a bit so it looks less flat. All I manage to do is charge my head with static electricity.

Great. Now I look like a cartoon character who stuck her finger in an electrical socket.

After carefully smoothing my hair down, I head back to my seat. Every row I pass is full. Makes sense. We're only ten days from Christmas; everyone's flying around the world at this time of year.

I squeeze past Aiden's legs and slide into my seat as he says, "You're just in time. I could feel the heart palpitations getting ready to attack me."

I roll my eyes. "You can tell your heart palpitations to save their energy for when the turbulence comes. Then they'll have something to get excited about."

Aiden's eyes widen ever so slightly.

"Um, I mean, turbulence isn't that bad." I tug my sleeves down over my hands—one of my nervous habits—as I look around, hoping the plane will provide me with inspiration. "Why do you think this seat is empty?" I say, gesturing to the open spot between us.

He raises an eyebrow. "Um, because no one booked it?"

"Every other row I passed is full. I've never flown at this time of year and had an empty seat next to me. I'm sure someone must have booked it."

"Maybe it was a businessman who finished a meeting late," Aiden suggests, "and then got stuck in rush-hour traffic and couldn't get to the airport on time."

"Maybe. That sounds a little boring, though."

Aiden raises an eyebrow. "Okay. Perhaps the businessman decided to take a taxi instead of the Tube because he had a big suitcase with him, but the taxi broke down."

"And as he stood on the side of the road trying to hail another taxi, he was abducted by aliens who took him to a parallel dimension."

Aiden's eyebrows climb a little higher. "Or maybe he managed to make it to the airport just in time, but as he was running, he tripped over an old lady's walking stick, knocked himself unconscious on the floor, and didn't hear the airport announcer person calling his name."

"And no one stopped to help him because a sneaky alien security guard dragged him into a private corridor to start experimenting on him."

Aiden shakes his head and laughs. "Why do there have to be aliens in this story?"

"Because that makes it more interesting. Why does the main character have to be a man?"

"Okay, it was a business*woman*. She got to the airport early, so she went to one of the restaurants to get dinner. She met a good-looking guy, started chatting, and didn't realise how fast the time went by—"

"Because her watch stopped working due to her latent supernatural ability that began to reveal itself a few days ago." I lean a little closer as my mind races ahead, filling in fantastical details. "And it wasn't a coincidence that the good-looking guy met her at the restaurant. He was waiting for her so he could tell her about the secret organisation of superheroes her father was a part of before he died. And now that her abilities are revealing themselves, she's been invited to join the organisation. So that's where she went instead of getting on the plane."

Aiden stares blankly at me for several seconds, then shrugs. "Okay, we can go with that. It's far more exciting than any of my theories."

I give him a shy smile as heat crawls up my neck. Most people I know roll their eyes at me when I start making up stories, so it's a nice change to have someone call them 'exciting'—even if what he's *thinking* may be entirely different.

Just as the silence between us starts to reach awkward point, Aiden says, "So, you're a sci-fi and fantasy fan? I thought at first you were more into the romantic chick stuff." He gestures towards the seat pocket in front of him where the top of my pink book is sticking out.

"Oh, no, not really. That's my sister's book. I took two of my own books with me, but I finished them faster than I thought I would. They were both paranormal-type stories."

"Do you think all that stuff is real?" Aiden asks. "Parallel dimensions and supernatural abilities and all that."

I narrow my eyes. Is he making fun of me?

"What? It's a genuine question," he says. "You believe in God, so maybe you believe in all things fantastical."

"And you don't."

He shrugs. "I'm a scientist. I don't need an entity I can't

see, hear, or touch if science and logic can explain everything for me."

"Not *everything*," I say as I twist my sleeves around my fingers. "And life isn't always about things you can see or hear or touch. Sometimes it's more than that."

Aiden leans across the empty seat and lowers his voice. "Like the feeling of security that settles over you when your guardian angel is nearby, brandishing a flaming, supernatural sword and fighting off the demons that threaten to steal your soul."

I stick my tongue out and push him back into his seat.

Laughing, he says, "You see? You're not the only one who can make up fantasy stories."

"Not all fantasy stories are made up," I tell him. "And maybe the one you just joked about is truer than you think it is."

He spreads his arms out, palm up. "Show me the angel with the flaming sword, and I'll be happy to believe. Until then, I'll stick with my science."

"Science doesn't rule out a higher being," I argue, aware somewhere at the back of my mind that I'm in the middle of an intelligent conversation with someone I barely know *and I haven't blanked yet!* "I'm a scientist too, and learning about all the intricate workings of the universe and its inhabitants only makes me believe in God even more."

Aiden looks at me sideways, narrows his eyes, and opens his mouth. Then he closes it without saying anything. He shifts around in his seat and watches me for several moments. "You remind me of one of my friends. He's been trying to convince me to go with him to church for years."

"And you keep telling him the invisible entity doesn't work for you."

"Pretty much." He grins, and I notice a dimple in his left cheek. "So, what kind of scientist are you, Sarah?"

I look down at my lap. "Oh, well, I'm not technically a scientist *yet*. I've done one year of a BSc, so I guess you could call me a scientist-in-training."

"Okay, what kind of scientist do you *plan* to be?"

"Um ..." I hate it when people ask me this, because I never have a proper answer. "I'm not sure yet. Sometimes I don't know why I picked science." And I don't know why I said that. He doesn't need to know that I can't figure out what to do with my life.

"Pick something else then," Aiden says, as if changing degrees isn't a big deal. "Something that induces such passion in you that you'll even talk to strangers about it. Something that includes making up fantastical stories, if possible," he adds with a grin.

A faint smile crosses my lips. "Yeah, maybe." Which is code for Not Happening. I've already had this conversation with someone in the past month, and it did *not* go well. Sticking with science is my safest option right now, especially since the only thing I feel any kind of passion for also happens to be something I suck at. "What about you?" I ask. "You can't be a real scientist yet either; you don't have wild hair and an uncontrollable beard."

"If that's a prerequisite for being a scientist, then you're going to have a problem."

"I know. I've been trying to grow a beard for months, but nothing will happen." I stroke my chin.

"And your hair is far too pretty to be considered wild."

Pretty? Oh my goodness, is he *flirting* with me? "You should have seen it just now in the bathroom," I say before allowing myself to get embarrassed. "I definitely would have been classified as *crazy scientist* with all that static electricity whizzing across my head."

With a smile, Aiden says, "I bet you still looked cute."

Oookay. I'm not an expert in this area, but I'm almost certain he's flirting with me. I grab a pamphlet from the seat pocket in front of me. "Have—have you seen the menu?" I open it up and pretend to peruse it so I won't have to look at Aiden. "The food's actually pretty good on this airline. I had salmon on the way here."

"Mmm, lamb brochette," Aiden says, leaning over to read my menu. "Looks good."

I focus on the words and instruct my brain to make sense of them. It's difficult, though, with Aiden leaning so close I can smell his deodorant or cologne or whatever it is he's wearing. Which makes me wonder what I smell like. Hopefully more like fruit—from Julia's cherry something-or-other shampoo I used this morning—and less like the cheese muffin I snacked on while waiting at the airport.

"How do you order food if you can't talk to strangers?" Aiden asks. "Sign language? Pointing?"

I roll my eyes. "I don't have a problem ordering food. It's not like I'm expected to have a detailed discussion with a waiter about the finer points of his life when all I need to say is, 'I'll have the smoked chicken salad, please.'"

"Right. No sign language then."

"No."

He pulls away from me—finally—and I can breathe easily once more. "So what's our entertainment line-up for the evening?" he asks as he touches the screen in front of him. "There must be at least one good movie on here."

"More than one." I touch the menu of my own screen. "They often show new releases." I navigate to the sci-fi movie I tried to get Julia to watch with me before I realised how much more expensive a movie ticket is in London than back home. "Does this mean I'm off the conversation-hook for the rest of the flight?"

"Of course not. Who says you can't talk during a movie?"

"Oh no. You're one of those?"

"I am one of those."

"My best friend is like that." I pull my headphones out of the seat pocket and unwind the cord. "It's one thing when you're on the couch at home, but when you're in the cinema? Yeah, it gets embarrassing. Someone threw popcorn at us once."

"Brilliant. Free popcorn." Aiden locates his headphones.

"Ew, are you serious? Would you really eat popcorn when you don't know whose hands have been all over it?"

"I might. In fact, if you were there, I definitely would. Just to see your reaction."

My fingers still on the headphone cord as I meet Aiden's gaze. I imagine the two of us sitting in a cinema together. In the semi-darkness. Our eyes locked the way they seem to be locked right now.

Whoa. I blink and look down. I plug my headphones in. I should *not* be thinking about Aiden in that way. Not when I have Matt.

But do I have Matt?

Honestly … I have no idea.

Stop thinking about Matt! He doesn't deserve to have any more thoughts or tears wasted on him.

"Good choice," Aiden says, and for a crazy second I think my inner pep-talk voice spoke out loud. Then I realise he's looking at the movie I selected. "Don't start it yet. I'll find the same one. We can critique it together." His fingers move quickly across his screen. He puts the headphones on, positioning them so that one ear is covered and one is free. "Ready?" he asks.

The image of Matt splinters into hundreds of pieces that drift away on an imaginary breeze. I smile at Aiden. "Yes."

I'M NOT A FILM CRITIC. I LIKE TO SIT BACK AND LET THE soundtrack wash over me and the story weave its way through my imagination. I like to lose myself for an hour or two. Aiden, however, can't shut up. He has a comment about everything, from the special effects to the actors chosen for the various roles to the fact that the 'science' makes little or no sense. It could be that I'm still somewhat mesmerised by his accent, but I find that I don't mind the interruptions.

Three hours later, after stopping the movie to order drinks, then dinner, and then pausing at least twenty times to argue about some detail or other, we finally finish. The cabin lights are dimmed, and most passengers are either sleeping or plugged into their screens. I slide my feet out of my shoes and reach for the aeroplane blanket I shoved under my chair earlier. I pull my knees up onto the seat and wrap the blanket around them.

"Okay, so that wasn't exactly an Oscar winner," I say. I take a sip of Chardonnay from my plastic wine glass before replacing it on the tray table between Aiden and me. "I'm glad I didn't pay to watch it in a cinema."

"Thank goodness I was here to give you a detailed commentary and dissection," Aiden says. "You might have fallen asleep other—"

Our smooth flight shifts abruptly to a bumpy one as turbulence rocks the plane.

Aiden swears loudly and grips the armrests of his chair. "What the hell was that?"

"Um, that would be turbulence."

"Turbulence? That felt like an aeroplane-sized pothole."

Another shudder ripples through the plane, stronger this time.

"Holy hell," Aiden gasps as I grab both our drinks before they start dancing towards the edge of the tray table. "So when you told me that everything in between taking off and landing is fine, you were lying."

"Not intentionally." I hold the drinks up as my seat bounces around. "I just … forgot about the turbulence part. And technically I think 'holy hell' might be an oxymoron. Since, you know, hell is bad. Not holy."

"Not helping."

"Well, at least you know for next time."

"Sarah!" He gives me the we're-all-gonna-die look.

"Hey, it's okay, this is normal." I tip back the last of my wine so I can put the glass down and place my hand over his. "Turbulence happens. The plane shakes around a bit, sometimes the seatbelt light comes back on, and then it passes and we all get on with sleeping or watching a movie or whatever. Just pretend you're on some kind of carnival ride instead of in a plane."

"Uh huh," Aiden says, but his eyes are squeezed shut and I can tell he doesn't believe me.

With one final shudder that knocks my glass over and sends the remaining ice block skittering across the tray table, the turbulence passes. I wait a few moments to make sure it's really gone, then say, "See? That wasn't so bad. They didn't even ask us to put our seatbelts on."

Aiden stares straight ahead, his breathing a little heavier than normal. I realise my hand is covering his. Crumbs, when did I do that? I barely know this guy and now I'm holding his hand? I lift the offending hand away from his and hide it in my lap. I'm still holding his drink, so I put that down too. I scoop the runaway ice block back into my glass and notice that Aiden still hasn't said anything. I look up, but he's watching the aisle. The tops of his ears are red.

"Um, are you okay?" I ask. Still he refuses to look at me. "Okay, so, I hope you're not embarrassed or anything. I mean, turbulence is scary if you don't know what to expect. I'm the real freak here, remember? The one who's scared of social interaction with perfectly harmless people." I laugh to let him know I'm joking. Trying to lighten the mood.

"It is embarrassing, though," he says quietly, his gaze still focused on the aisle. "That kid over there didn't even put her iPad down."

"Well, you know, she's probably too engrossed in catapulting birds at pigs or something. If she were even remotely aware of her surroundings, I'm sure she would have been scared too."

Aiden gives me a small smile. "I doubt it. But thanks anyway. And thanks for saving my wine. When you start off with such a tiny drink, it would suck to lose half of it."

I laugh. "It would. We should start a petition for larger aeroplane cups."

"Yes. Right after I figure out where my blanket is. Where'd you get yours from?"

"It was on my chair when I got here."

"Which means I'm probably sitting on mine." Aiden reaches beneath his butt—*don't think about his butt!*—and pulls out an aeroplane pillow.

"How did you *not* know you were sitting on that?" I ask.

"Is this what they call a pillow?"

"I'm afraid it is."

"Ridiculous. How is anyone supposed to get a good night's sleep on this pincushion? I should have bought one of those blow-up pillows that wrap around your neck."

"Are you planning to sleep now?" I try to keep the disappointment out of my voice. I'm tired, but—as insane as it is for me to admit this—I'd rather stay awake and talk to Aiden.

"After that turbulence?" Aiden shakes his head as he pulls his blanket out from beneath him. "Not a chance. However," he adds, "if I'm about to die, perhaps it would be better if I didn't know it was coming."

"We're not about to die."

Aiden drapes his blanket over his legs and pulls it up to his lap. It's exactly what most people do when they're flying overnight, but somehow it looks cuter on him. Like he's all ready for bed now. "If we were about to die, though," he says, "what's one thing you wouldn't miss?"

"Hmm." I wrap my arms around my knees and pull them closer. "Going back to varsity. I'm not too excited about that."

"Which one are you at?"

I give him a sideways look. "Not the one you're thinking of."

"How do you know which one I'm thinking of?"

"Because people from other countries only ever know about one South African university."

He hesitates before saying, "Okay. Guilty as charged. I only know the Cape Town one."

"Exactly."

"So you don't go there?"

"Nope." The prospect of travelling across the country to study at a massive university with thousands of people I don't know was just a little too terrifying for me. I opted for the small campus an hour away from home and the tiny garden flat in my mom's old school friend's back garden. And it didn't hurt that Matt had already chosen to go there ...

Get out of my head, Matt!

I blink and find Aiden watching me. "What?"

"Just waiting to see if you'll carry on talking if I don't

31

ask you anything else."

The dreaded blush creeps up my neck again. "Okay, you see? This is the problem. I *want* to keep talking to you, but any time it's my turn to bring up a new topic of conversation, my brain can't seem to pick anything."

"So ask me a question."

Right. That's the normal thing to do. You get to know people by asking them questions. If I could stop being so self-conscious, maybe I'd remember that. "Um … tell me three random things about yourself."

"That's not exactly a question."

"I know. But right now my brain is stuck at 'What don't you like to eat' and 'How many siblings do you have,' both of which are super boring. So I'm trusting you'll come up with something more interesting than that."

Aiden puts both hands behind his head and stares at the seat in front of him. "Uh, okay. One, the best Christmas present I ever got was a pair of rollerblades. I spent every day after school going up and down the road outside our house until my mom confiscated them so I'd do my homework. Two, I wanted to be a magician when I was growing up. And three, I think happily ever afters are a myth." He twists his head to look at me. "And in answer to your boring questions, I don't eat fish and I have one older sister. Your turn."

"Wait." I hold my hand up. "Why are happily ever afters a myth?"

He shrugs. "They just are. Now you tell me your random three things."

I want to prod further, find out why exactly he doesn't believe this 'myth.' But I'm too scared to push in case this is an off-limits topic for him. If that were the case, though, he wouldn't have brought it up, would he?

"Sarah?"

"Um, right." I chicken out. "My three things are … One, I'm addicted to zoo biscuits. Two, I used to act out stories to my friends using Barbie dolls as the main characters. And three, my older sister is a talented photographer, my younger sister is an amazing artist, and I don't have a creative bone in my body."

"You don't?" Aiden looks pointedly at the empty seat between us. "I think the businesswoman who missed her flight because she discovered her supernatural abilities and was invited to join a secret organisation of superheroes would disagree."

I shake my head. "That's not the same thing. Silly stories don't count. You should see what my sisters can do. Julia's won awards with her photographs, and Sophie's art is so incredible she has thousands of fans on online, some of whom buy her work from her. She's only fifteen! And here I am, the unremarkable middle daughter whom no one ever remembers."

On the other side of the empty seat, Aiden's eyes widen.

Oh wow. Crap. I did NOT just say all of that out loud!

I did.

"So … turns out this might be a therapy session after all," Aiden says.

"No, no, no, I'm sorry. I shouldn't have said any of that.

My sisters are awesome and I love them and … I'm just sad about my holiday ending and because I don't know when I'll see Julia again." *And because in less than twenty-four hours I may have to face Matt.*

"You know, we've still got a couple of hours left of this flight," Aiden says, "so if you need to talk about—"

"No. Seriously. There's nothing to talk about. Forget what I said. The depressing parts, I mean. You can remember the rest of it. If you want. The happy stuff. The zoo biscuits and the Barbie dolls."

Ugh, I need to shut up.

Aiden twists in his seat so he's facing me, then leans his head against the seat. A half-smile lingers on his lips. "You intrigue me."

Blank.

Blank.

After what seems like an eternity, I manage a strangled giggle. "I—what? No I don't."

"You do."

"No. A girl with blue and purple streaks in her hair and weirdly shaped scars on her hands who hints that she may have been brought up on a pirate ship is intriguing. A girl who swears you to secrecy before telling you that her brilliant scientist parents are trying to prove time travel exists and she's on her way to witness them testing their very own time machine on a human for the first time is intriguing."

Aiden smiles, revealing that cute dimple of his again. "You have insane stories like that going on in your head all the time. That's pretty intriguing."

"Or just weird."

"I like weird.

"Well … I … like …" *Guys with messy hair, cute dimples, and charming British accents.*

DO NOT SAY THAT OUT LOUD!

"I guess I like weird too," I mumble.

"And you like biscuits from the zoo—whatever those may be."

"What? No, okay, zoo biscuits are not biscuits you get at the zoo. They're vanilla biscuits with a brightly coloured layer of hard icing on top of them and a white icing animal on top of that."

"Sounds healthy."

"They're not. My mom tells me my teeth are going to fall out every time she sees me eating them." I shrug. "I try to restrict my zoo biscuit intake. It's tough, though."

"You see?" Aiden says, his eyes twinkling. "Intriguing."

I groan. "I think I need to get you a dictionary for Christmas."

"Oh, we're exchanging Christmas presents now, are we? I was under the impression our relationship was going to last one flight—two, if we're on the same plane from Dubai to Durban—and then I'd never see you again. But if you want to get me a Christmas present—" a sexy grin slides onto his face "—we may have to arrange a secret rendezvous on Christmas Eve."

My breath catches somewhere between my lungs and my mouth as my brain processes Aiden's words. He's also going to Durban? What if I bump into him? What if he really *does* want to arrange a secret rendezvous? Would I say yes?

"Sarah? That was a joke."

Right. Of course. And there are more than three million other people in Durban, so bumping into him is unlikely. And a planned meeting wouldn't be a good idea because I'd just have to say goodbye to him in a few weeks when he returns home.

And there's Matt.

Possibly.

UGH!

Aiden leans over to pat my arm. "Relax. I won't force conversation on you any longer than I have to." He checks his watch. "Only a couple more hours."

"I'm also flying to Durban," I blurt out.

"Oh, great." His face lights up. He winks. "If you're really unlucky, we'll be on the same flight."

As it turns out, luck has it in for me: Aiden and I are on the same flight to Durban. Our seats are far apart, but if Aiden has anything to do with it, he'll figure out a way to fix that. Which means my conversation nightmare will continue for another eight hours and forty minutes. Only … it hasn't been a nightmare at all. More like one of those odd dreams where you wake up feeling happy and you can't figure out why because the vivid wisps of dream are already fading, but you know there was something amazing about it.

"Okay, we've got about two and a half hours to shop up a storm before we need to board the next flight," I say to Aiden as we ride the final escalator up into Dubai International Airport's duty-free shopping area. We join the throng of passengers pushing trolleys, pulling suitcases, and perusing electronics, scarves, nuts and a hundred other things for sale. Different accents and languages weave through the air around us, mingling with the overpowering scent of too many perfumes.

"Is it always this busy?" Aiden asks. His backpack is slung over his shoulder, and he's pulling my wheeled carry-on suitcase behind him.

I tuck my handbag securely beneath my arm; this is a pickpocket's paradise. "I think so. I've only been here once before—on the way to England—but it was just like this."

We weave our way between a group of Americans and an Asian family and head towards an electronics stand. "This stuff doesn't look that cheap," Aiden says, eyeing the price next to the demo model of the latest Kindle.

"It isn't. At least, not when I convert it to rands." My hand hovers over a sleek new tablet, but I decide against touching it when I notice the multitude of fingerprints covering the screen. I tuck my hands into the safety of my hoodie's pocket. "What does work out to be cheaper, though, are some brands of chocolate. So I'll probably be spending my remaining English money on that."

"Good plan," Aiden says. "I hear chocolate can solve just about any problem when you're a girl."

After sticking my tongue out at him, I pull him away from the overpriced gadgets. We wander through the shops, looking at jewellery, clothes, food, watches, cosmetics—at least, I examine the cosmetics while Aiden stands in a queue to pay for our stash of chocolates—shoes, books, cameras and more. By the time we reach the Häagen-Dazs stand, I'm overheating in my hoodie and tired of fighting the crowds.

"Is it a good time for ice cream?" I ask.

Aiden gives me a look that I think is supposed to say, *Duh.* "It's always a good time for ice cream."

"That can't possibly be true." We make our way towards the Häagen-Dazs counter. "Not when you live in one of the coldest places on earth."

"Um, I should probably point out that there are far colder places than the UK. Like Alaska. And Russia."

"Okay, look." I rest my hip against the counter. "Having lived in a subtropical climate my entire life, England was the coldest place I've ever experienced. Not to mention grey, wet, and depressing. I have no idea why Julia wants to live there."

"You should see it in summer." Aiden leans a little closer to me. "It's beautiful."

Don't stare, don't stare. I clear my throat, then start digging in my handbag for my foreign money. "You got the chocolate," I say without looking at him, "so this one's on me. What flavour do you want?"

"Hmm. Surprise me," Aiden says, then drags my suitcase to a table nearby and sits down.

I choose a classic flavour for myself—chocolate chip cookie dough—and go with something more exotic for Aiden—pineapple coconut. As I head back to the table, Aiden frowns at something in his hand. His cell phone. I slide into the chair opposite him and wonder if I should say something, but the frown vanishes from his face as he pushes the phone into his front jeans pocket.

"So, what delicious flavour will I be devouring today?" he asks.

I hand him his tub, and he raises an eyebrow. "What? You asked for a surprise. That's a surprise."

"It certainly is." He removes the cap and digs in with his plastic spoon while I wipe the section of table in front of me with a serviette. I definitely don't want to lean my elbows on that sticky mark I saw there. "Mm, this is amazing," he says.

"Really? Let me try."

"No way. You made your choice. You have to live with cookie dough now." He holds his ice cream out of reach, but I lean across the table and manage to get my spoon into the tub.

"Thief," he says as I settle back in my chair, carefully bringing the plastic spoon towards my mouth.

"Whatever. You know you want some of—No!" The stolen blob of ice cream lands on my hoodie, right in the centre of the R in BOOK FREAK.

"You see?" Aiden says, giving me a superior look. "Thieves never prosper."

"It's *cheaters* never prosper, silly." I attempt to scrape the ice cream off my hoodie. A wet patch remains. "Ew, now I have to go wash this."

"Not really," Aiden says. "It's hardly dirty."

"I, um, have a thing about … mess. Sticky stuff and dirty stuff and … you know." I dab at the wet patch with a serviette.

"So your hoodie should actually say CLEAN FREAK instead of BOOK FREAK?"

"It should probably say CLEAN FREAK *and* BOOK FREAK. And several other kinds of freak too."

"If I were wearing a hoodie," Aiden says between mouthfuls of pineapple coconut ice cream, "what would my freak label be?"

"Um …" I eat a few scoops of chocolate chip cookie dough while thinking. "MAGIC FREAK."

He gives me a questioning look.

"What, you said you wanted to be a magician."

"Yeah, like fifteen years ago."

"ROLLERBLADE FREAK?"

"Not even close."

"MYTH BUSTER FREAK."

"You're insane."

We argue about freak names for Aiden until I've finished my tub of ice cream. Then I push my chair back, pull out the extendable handle of my carry-on suitcase, and make sure my handbag is zipped up. "Okay, I'm going to find a bathroom."

"What, you don't trust me with your hand luggage?" Aiden asks. "You think I'm gonna run off with your regulation-sized toiletries and the stash of chocolates you stuffed in there just now?"

"Those were high quality chocolates. You can't be trusted with them." I try to keep a straight face as I turn and walk away, but it proves impossible.

After weaving through the crowds and running over a child's foot with my suitcase—which earns me a very dirty look from the child's mother, despite my numerous stuttered apologies—I manage to find a bathroom. I wait in line for what feels like far too long, then drag my suitcase over to a basin when it becomes available. Since I have to change my hoodie, I may as well take a few minutes to wash my face and freshen up a bit.

You wouldn't bother if Aiden weren't with you, a voice at the back of my mind whispers. Which isn't true, because I like to be clean, so how does that silly voice know I wouldn't freshen up if I were travelling alone?

I locate my bag of tiny toiletries and start my cleansing routine, trying not to look at the woman next to me who appears to be giving herself a sponge bath. She's stripped down to her underwear and is patting herself all over with a star-shaped orange sponge, apparently oblivious to the people around her.

Man, I wish I were that confident.

And I hope I look that good when I'm her age.

Okay, focus. Freshen up and find clean clothes. I finish at the basin, then crouch down and search through my neatly packed suitcase. Beneath the toiletries and chocolates are the clothes I couldn't fit into my main suitcase. I pull out the grey-and-white striped jersey I borrowed from Julia and decided to keep after she said it looked better on me. I remove the ice cream hoodie, pull on the jersey—and get a face-full of Sponge Bath Lady's backside.

I scoot backwards before the butt—complete with a tattooed pattern of symbols just above it—can make contact with my face. I consider telling the woman she almost knocked me over with her rear, but I decide it's not worth the risk. Who knows how she'll respond? She might be rude, and then I'll go blank and stumble out of here like a total moron.

Perfume. Find perfume. Yes, right, that's what I was going to do before I was almost shoved in the face by a pair of lacy panties. I spritz my wrists and neck and breathe in the fresh, aquatic scent while considering the symbols on Sponge Bath Lady's tattoo. I don't recognise them, but they're kind of … exotic looking. I wish I knew what they meant. I wish I were brave enough to ask her.

The cogs of my imagination start turning, working through maybes and what-ifs to concoct a wild story all starting with that tattoo. Sponge Bath Lady is part of a secret organisation. Just like the man who met the businesswoman in the airport restaurant to explain her special abilities to her. To explain that she is one of the Gifted. But this is a different organisation. An evil one. They've figured out how to steal special abilities, and now they hunt down unsuspecting Gifted who don't even know what they can do yet. And that pattern of weird symbols is what they brand their Hunters with. Which makes Sponge Bath Lady a Hunter. She's searching for the businesswoman—and her hunt has only just begun.

After a quick glance at my watch—I still have time—I push my hand beneath my clothes and feel the hard edges of a notebook and pen at the bottom of my suitcase. I ignored the notebook the entire time I was away, but perhaps it's time to add to it. I pull it out, sit down on top of the suitcase, and flip quickly to a blank page. I start scribbling down details. Scenes play out across the backdrop of my imagination as I write. I've even figured out the perfect ending.

When I reach the end of my inspirational rush, I slide the notebook back into my suitcase. Sponge Bath Lady is gone, and I don't recognise any of the other people lined up at the basins. I guess I was writing longer than I thought, but my watch still says I have plenty of time until we need to board.

I push through crowds once more until I see the Häagen-Dazs sign and Aiden sitting in a chair. His back is to me, but he's the only guy there, so I know it's him. It looks like he's changed his jacket, though. And I'm sure his hair isn't that light …

Hang on. That's not Aiden.

I stop outside the Häagen-Dazs area and look around, but I don't see him anywhere. Okay. Weird. Maybe he also needed to go to the bathroom. I lean against the handle of my suitcase and check my watch.

Wait. WAIT. The hands are in the same position they were in when I pulled out my notebook. The same position they were in when I left the bathroom.

My watch has stopped working.

CRAP! How long was I in there? Panic drenches me in goose bumps. My fingers scramble through my handbag, searching for my phone. I feel the hard, smooth edges and pull it out. It's on aeroplane mode, so there should be plenty of battery life left. My shaking thumb presses a button, and the screen lights up. The moment I see the numbers, my churning stomach drops down to my feet. The gate I'm supposed to board at closes in two minutes.

5

I START RUNNING, WHICH IS DIFFICULT WITH THE AMOUNT of people around me. I'm supposed to be at gate … gate … Dammit, I'm usually so good with remembering numbers. I manage to pull my ticket out of my handbag while still running. I see the nearest gate. Despite the panicked state of my brain, I manage to do the math. My gate is nine away from here.

I start running faster.

Six more to go.

Three more to go.

There it is!

I run down the empty ramp towards the desk and the two uniformed women who look like they may be about to leave. "Wait!" I yell. "Am I too late?"

One of them sighs as I reach the desk. "Almost too late," she says in an accent I can't identify. "But not quite." She holds out her hand for my ticket.

"Oh, thank goodness," I pant. I hand over my ticket, then dig in my handbag for my passport. I hand it to the second woman, who looks a lot friendlier than the first.

"Oh, you're the one that guy kept asking us about," she says when she opens my passport. She sounds South African—Afrikaans, possibly—which is such a comfort right now that I almost start crying.

"S-someone was asking about me?"

"Yes. He kept saying he had to wait for you. We forced him to board a few minutes ago." She smiles. "He'll be very happy to see you."

Tears burn behind my eyes, and I take a deep breath and blink them away. I walk down the corridor as quickly as my shaking legs will allow. Once on the plane, I divide my attention between searching for my seat and searching for Aiden. I can't remember where he's sitting; I was going to leave it up to him to make a plan for us to sit together.

People are watching me. I might be imagining it, but they seem annoyed. Did I do something wrong? I find my seat—in between an overweight man reading a newspaper and a teen girl who looks like she's already asleep—but the compartment above it is already full. I open three other compartments before finding space for my suitcase.

And people don't stop staring for a second.

By the time I squeeze past the man and drop into my seat, my face is burning. Why, *why* did I have to start writing in that notebook? These stupid stories of mine have given me nothing but trouble. I should gather up every notebook

I have and throw them all away. Or burn them. That might be more satisfying.

I rub my eyes, and my head throbs as a wave of utter exhaustion rolls over me. Hardly surprising considering it's about six in the morning in London and I didn't sleep all night. I dig inside my handbag and pull out my phone and the small drawstring bag that contains my flattened travel pillow. I press a button on the phone's screen and check the time. Yip, it's almost six thirty in the morning in London. *Far* too many hours since I last slept. With a great deal of effort—my lungs seem to be as exhausted as the rest of my body—I manage to blow up the pillow. I fit it around my neck. Then, still clutching my phone, I cross my arms and close my eyes. I'll sleep for a little bit, just until they bring the drinks trolley around, or the next meal, and then I'll search the aisles to see if I can find Aiden.

I wake abruptly from a dream in which I'm running through a crowded airport trying to catch Julia. My neck aches and my throat is horribly dry, but I don't feel nearly as tired as I did when I first sat down. I blink a few times and wipe my hand over my mouth. Is that dried saliva on my chin? I find my phone lying face down on my lap—thank goodness no one stole it—and turn it over to check the time. I blink once more. Oh my *heck*, have I seriously been asleep for seven hours? No wonder I don't feel tired anymore. I've got less than two hours left on this plane.

Ugh. I don't want to be back in Durban.

And Aiden! I have to find him and tell him I made it onto the plane!

"Afternoon, Book Freak. Did you sleep well?"

I jerk to the side in fright as the person in the aisle seat leans towards me.

Aiden.

What? How did he get there?

Oh, crumbs, how awful do I look right now? I rub hastily at my chin, hoping to remove all traces of drool. I open my mouth to speak, then snap it shut. After seven hours of sleep, I probably have the most horrendous morning breath. And my hair—it's all bunched up around my neck because of that silly blow-up pillow. Why does Aiden have to sit next to me *now*? And how? What happened to the overweight man with the newspaper?

Wait. Maybe I'm still asleep.

"You look confused," Aiden says, then narrows his eyes. "Or is that your scared face? Because if it is, I'm starting to think you deserted me in the airport on purpose." He leans back. "You know, if you detested my company that much, you should have just said so."

"I—I'm so sorry," I stutter, my hand fluttering near my mouth to try and shield him from the dragon breath. "I lost track of time while I was in the bathroom."

His eyebrows shoot up. "Really? You lost track of *that much* time? Okay, now I'm almost certain you left me on purpose." He unclips his seatbelt. "But don't worry. We can fix this. I'm sure the chubby gentleman will be happy to trade seats with me again. However," he adds, "he may think it rather strange that after begging him to let me sit next to my sick sister to make sure she takes all her medication, I'm now abandoning her."

"I—your sick sister?"

"Yes. You contracted the Millicent virus while we were on holiday. You became delirious in the airport, which is why you ran away from me."

I take a few moments to process Aiden's words before responding. "I'm guessing the chubby gentleman was quick to leave after that."

"He was."

"I'm also guessing there's no such thing as the Millicent virus."

"Well, that's debatable. I had a horrid old aunt named Millicent. She was always cooking up disgusting concoctions in her kitchen. One of them could have been a virus."

"Right. Did you tell the chubby gentleman that part as well?"

"Oh no. He heard the words 'virus' and 'delirious' and that was all it took for him to shoot up out of this seat. Poor man's probably never moved so fast."

I start laughing, then cover my mouth when I remember the dragon breath. "Well, congratulations on coming up with such an exciting story."

Aiden inclines his head. "Thank you, but it was all you. I was inspired by your wild imagination."

I close my eyes and groan. "It's my wild imagination that almost caused me to miss this flight. I started writing down a story in my notebook while I was in the bathroom, and my watch stopped working so I didn't realise how long I was taking." I pull my sleeve back and show Aiden my watch as proof. "So I really am sorry for abandoning you in the airport. I looked out for you when I got onto the plane, but I couldn't see you anywhere. I was just going to have a quick nap and then look for you, but ... I guess that didn't happen."

"Well, it's a good thing I remembered your seat number," Aiden says, "otherwise I might still be picturing you hiding out at the airport, so desperate to get away from me that you were willing to miss a flight for it."

I laugh and consider slapping his arm playfully, but I don't think I'm cool enough to pull that off. "How long have you been sitting next to me?"

"Uh ... since the seatbelt light first went off."

"What?" Embarrassment heats my cheeks. "Why didn't you wake me?"

"Well, I was tired," Aiden says with a shrug. "I figured since you were sleeping, I might as well sleep too."

"You don't look like you've been sleeping. *I* look like I've been sleeping, but you look perfectly groomed."

"Do I, now?" His sexy grin makes a reappearance. "And how would you know what I look like when I've been sleeping?"

"I ... I didn't mean ..." Flustered, I pull the blow-up pillow away from my neck—why didn't I do that when I

51

first woke up?—and reach for my handbag. "I need to go to the bathroom."

Aiden bursts out laughing. "You can't keep escaping to the bathroom, Sarah."

"But I actually need to go this time!" I protest.

"Oh, so when you told me you needed to go on the last flight, you were lying?"

"I—no—just let me past, please."

Aiden moves his legs aside with a sigh, and I hurry away before I embarrass myself further.

In the tiny bathroom, I neaten up my hair as much as I can without getting the electrified look before rubbing some fruity scented cream on my hands and neck. Perfume might be better, but I left it in my suitcase in one of the overhead compartments. I pull out my travel sized toothbrush and toothpaste and get to work ridding myself of dragon breath. Julia thought it was hilarious that I bothered to get a travel toothbrush, but she'd be grateful if she were in this situation.

I get back to my row to find Aiden holding a phone that looks far too familiar. "Hey, that's mine." I squeeze past him, dump my handbag on the floor, and sit down. "Hand it over."

"What, I thought you left it on your seat specifically for me to look at."

My chest constricts as I think of all the whacky and embarrassing photos I took over the past three weeks. "What exactly did you look at?"

"Relax, Book Freak. I was just looking at your

background photo. Is that your sister? The one you were visiting?"

I breathe a sigh of relief. "Yes, that's Julia." I take the phone from him and look at the picture of Julia and me puckering our lips for a selfie with Big Ben in the background. It's ridiculous how much I miss her already.

"She's the photographer?" Aiden asks.

"Yes." I lock my phone and slide it back into my handbag. "Sophie is The Artist Daughter and Julia is The Photographer Daughter. Formerly known as The Perfect Daughter."

"Formerly?"

"Yes. She kinda lost that label after she ran away from home and didn't contact anyone for almost a year."

"Really?" Aiden looks at me to check whether I'm joking.

"Really."

"Wow. I mean, there were times I wanted to run away, but I never actually did it."

"Yeah." I pull my knees up to my chest. "My parents were really upset."

"Understandably. That sounds a little …"

"What?"

"Well, a little selfish. Running off and not contacting anyone. I could never do that to my mum. She'd be devastated."

"I guess." I trace invisible patterns across my knee. "Julia had a good reason for it, though."

"It must have been something big."

"It was."

"Was it to do with your parents?"

I shake my head.

"So why ignore them for so long?"

I take a deep breath. "It was … complicated. A whole lot of things. And my parents were too distracted by their own work to notice any of it. My dad's an overworked high school teacher and my mom runs a lab at a biotech company. I mean, they're good parents, but they get really busy and then they miss a lot of stuff. So when The Big Thing happened right after Julia's finals, I think something inside her just … snapped. So she left."

I look up to see if Aiden gets what I'm trying to say. I know it shouldn't matter what he thinks of my sister, but for some reason, I care about his opinion.

"How did you two end up close then?" he asks. "I assume you're close, since you just spent three weeks with her and you didn't want to leave."

"I kept sending her emails after she left. Eventually she started responding. I think she liked that I wrote about random stuff. Everyone else wanted to know why she left and where exactly she was and when she was planning to come home. I figured she didn't want to talk about that, so I didn't ask. Anyway, somehow I ended up feeling closer to her after she left than I ever did when she lived at home. So in a weird sort of way, I'm glad she ran away."

Aiden nods. "I used to be close to my sister like that."

"But not anymore?"

He shakes his head, but doesn't elaborate.

"I'm sorry," I say. "Here I am rambling on about my family, and I haven't asked you anything about yours."

"There isn't much to say. It's just me, my mum, and my sister."

"And all the relatives you're meeting up with in South Africa."

"And all of them."

I notice he doesn't say anything about his father. Should I ask? Would it be rude to ask? Would it be rude *not* to ask? Ugh, how did I become so socially inept?

"Tell me about your other sister, Sophie," Aiden says, changing the subject.

So I tell him about Sophie's paintings and her digital art and her beautifully detailed doodles, and before I know it, we're beginning our descent. My stomach drops along with the plane. Aiden becomes more anxious on the outside— fingers tapping, knees bouncing—and I become more anxious on the inside. The ground grows closer. Closer. Closer.

Touchdown.

I<small>T SMELLS LIKE HOME. IT FEELS LIKE HOME. THE AIR ISN'T</small>
just warmer, it's almost … thicker. Fuller. Heavy with
moisture. The moment my feet touch the runway surface, I
pull off my jersey. No doubt I'll be complaining about the
heat and humidity soon enough, but for now I relish the feel
of late afternoon sun on my skin. I imagine drawing the
moisture-filled air closer around me like an old, comforting
blanket.

And I try not to think about Matt.

Inside the airport, we're directed towards passport
control. South African passengers on one side; foreign
passengers on the other. As Aiden separates from my side to
join the rest of the foreigners, the terrifying thought that I
may never see him again paralyzes me for a moment.

"See you on the other side," he says cheerfully, squeezing
my arm before stepping away from me. "Look out for my

suitcase. It has a bright pink ribbon on it."

Relieved, I start laughing. "You joke," I say, "but my suitcase actually does have a pink ribbon tied to it."

I wait for what feels like forever in the South African queue, watching the short foreigner queue rapidly getting shorter. After Aiden disappears on the other side of the passport counter, I grow more and more agitated. If his suitcase comes through before mine, what reason does he have to wait for me? If the person fetching him sends a message to say they're waiting, he'd have to leave, wouldn't he? And he'd have no way to let me know. He'd disappear into the crowded airport and I'd never see him again. Of course, I'll probably never see him again after today anyway, but I still want to say goodbye.

When I've finally had my passport checked by a thoroughly disinterested woman, I hurry through to the baggage claim area, dragging my carry-on suitcase behind me. I get myself a trolley, lift my small bag onto it, and push it towards the correct carousel as quickly as I can. Of course, I managed to pick the trolley that has wonky wheels that keep trying to make me turn left, so it takes longer than it should.

After scanning the crowd for a while, I find Aiden lifting a dark blue duffel bag off the carousel. I steer my rebellious trolley towards him. "Oh, hey, you made it," he says when he looks up and sees me. "There's a plain black suitcase with a pink-and-white striped ribbon that's done a few rounds on the carousel. Might that be yours?"

"Yes, that's mine."

We wait for it to come around again, and Aiden hoists it onto my trolley. We steer our way through the people still waiting for their luggage and head towards the sliding doors, and even though these are my last few minutes with Aiden, I can't think of a single thing to say.

"So," he says, breaking the silence between us, "my loving aunt sent me a message just now to say she'll be at the pick-up area in twenty minutes, and that if I'm not there waiting for her, she'll leave without me."

"How welcoming of her."

"Indeed. Do you want to wait with me, or is someone coming inside for you?"

Yes, I want to wait with you!

We pass through the sliding doors and enter the sea of people waiting eagerly for their loved ones. I look down so I don't have to meet anyone's gaze. I hate how people stare hungrily every time those doors open. They're all watching, waiting, hoping. I don't want to see their disappointment when they realise I'm not the one they're waiting for.

"Um, sorry," I say to Aiden, remembering he asked me a question, "but my mom has this theory that the drop-off area is never as busy as the pick-up area, so she told me to wait up there for her."

"Okay." Is it my imagination, or does Aiden sound a little sad that I won't be waiting with him? "Is her theory correct?" he asks.

I shrug as we reach a quieter area next to an elevator and bring our trolleys to a halt. "Maybe. Probably."

"Moms know best, right?" he says with a wink.

"Yeah."

"Well, I guess this is goodbye, then."

"Uh huh." I match his smile and try to figure out a way to casually say something like, 'Hey, we should stay in contact. What's your number?' or 'Hey, are you on Facebook? We should connect,' without sounding like a needy stalker creep. But since I've never asked a guy for his number before, I'm not sure how to do it. How does everyone else do it? Do they just ask? Isn't that weird? Maybe I'm just weird.

"Sarah?" he says.

"Yeah?" I force myself to look up into his eyes.

"Why were you crying?"

My heart leaps up into my throat. "W-what?"

He watches me carefully. "When I first sat down on the plane, you were crying."

"I …" I swallow, trying to think of something to say. A joke. Denial. A way to lighten the suddenly serious atmosphere between us. But the look in his eyes is so genuine, so caring, that there's no way I can lie to him. I look down at my shoes. "I didn't want to come home," I say. "My life feels kind of messed up at the moment, and I didn't want to have to deal with … the people here."

I close my eyes. Fabulous. I can't very well ask him if he wants to stay in contact after admitting I'm a messed up freak. He'll probably nod slowly, write down a fake number, and back away as quickly as he can.

The next thing I feel is a pair of arms around me. Strong, yet gentle. Comforting. "Don't worry," Aiden says into my ear. "Everyone's life gets messed up sometimes. Look at me: I'm still figuring out how to be an aeroplane passenger without curling into the foetal position and rocking slowly while muttering 'Please don't explode' over and over." He withdraws his arms and steps away while I try to act naturally, as if guys I barely know hug me all the time and I'm totally cool with it. "Enjoy what holiday you still have left," he says, "and keep writing that book. The one you almost missed a flight for. I bet it'll be a bestseller one day."

He gives me one last grin, turns away, and heads towards the door that'll take him outside to the pick-up area. And I fight the urge to run after him screaming 'Please come back!' like a mad woman.

I watch him until he's gone. Then I take a deep breath, pull my phone out of my bag, unlock the screen, and stare at the picture of Jules and me. The phone is still on aeroplane mode, the way it's been for the entire time I was away. I wanted to use it for the camera and my music, but I didn't want to risk having any messages come through. I used Julia's computer to check email and Facebook a few times, and if Mom wanted to get hold of me, she contacted Julia. All my friends knew I was away, so they didn't expect me to reply to texts. The only person I really *did* want to hear from was also the person I really *didn't* want to hear from, which is the main reason my phone is still in non-communication mode.

Matt.

But I can't avoid him any longer. Plus I need to let my mother know I've landed and need a lift home.

I navigate to my phone settings and turn off aeroplane mode. Then I switch my phone to silent so I don't have to listen to all the dings and beeps and trills as my phone receives every email, text, Facebook notification, tweet and every other kind of message it missed over the last three weeks.

I grip my phone tightly in my hand and cross my arms. I watch the people around me as I let myself think about Matt for the first time since I left.

My boyfriend?

My ex-boyfriend?

How did I get to the point where I don't even know if Matt and I are still together? Worse still, how did I get to the point where I don't even know if I *want* to be with him anymore? If he stood in front of me right now and said, 'It's up to you, Sarah. Should we end this, or should we stay together?' I'd have no idea what to say.

I take another deep breath and force myself to look at my phone. I scroll through all the unread messages, my eyes searching for Matt's name.

Nothing. Not a single message.

I swallow, blink, and look around. I guess it really is over between us. I suppose it couldn't be any other way, not after the things we said to each other the night before I left. I try to figure out how I feel about our break-up—the end of a two-year relationship—but I can't feel much besides tiredness and a hint of nausea and that unmistakable *aloneness*.

I quickly type a message to my mom, then press the

elevator button. I slip the phone back into my handbag.

"Hey, you're still here."

Startled, I turn and find Aiden right beside me. "Hey. Yeah."

"I remembered I still have your book," he says, handing over the offensively pink novel. "I'd hate for you never to find out how it ends."

With my heart pounding in a way that makes my voice sound oddly breathless, I take hold of the book. "I've already predicted the ending, remember?"

His dimple shows up as he smiles. "But you still need to get to the end to make sure your predictions are correct."

"Of course."

I try to take the book from him, but he doesn't let go. He leans closer to me, tilting his head to the side a little.

Wait. What's happening? Is he—

His lips press firmly against mine.

And my brain blanks out yet again.

As if I have no control over my body, my eyes slide shut and my hand slips away from the trolley and finds Aiden's arm. My grip tightens—one hand on the book and the other fisted around his sleeve—and I pull myself closer to him, willing him never to let go, willing everyone around us to disappear, willing time itself to stand still.

All too soon, Aiden detaches himself from me and steps back. He smiles a smile I don't understand, turns, and hurries away. I sway a little and grab onto my trolley for support. Why is he leaving? Why didn't he *say* anything?

And where are his bags? He didn't leave them outside unattended, did he?

Without having decided to, I find myself pushing my trolley forwards. Faster and faster, wiggling from side to side as I fight with that STUPID wheel that wants me to turn left. I skid through the open doors and yank my trolley to a halt. My eyes flick across the waiting cars and travellers, barely seeing anything as I search for that *one person* with the dark hair and the tan jacket and—

I see him. Climbing into a car. Pulling the door shut.

The car moves forwards. Away. Around the corner.

Gone.

I let out a long breath, deflating like a popped balloon. This makes NO sense. Who kisses someone like that and then *doesn't say anything*? What am I supposed to do now? What did it mean? Unless … unless it wasn't supposed to mean anything. Unless it was just a crazy goodbye.

I look down and find I'm still holding the pink book in one hand—probably one of the reasons I was struggling to push the trolley straight. I slide it inside my handbag and turn the trolley around. I head slowly back inside and wait by the elevator until the doors glide open. The elevator carries me upward while I play that kiss over and over in my mind. I can barely believe I did that. It took me three dates before I worked up the courage to let Matt close enough for a kiss, yet there I was not only *letting* a guy I hardly know kiss me, but kissing him back. Pulling him closer. Not wanting it to end.

I push my trolley out of the elevator, across the airport

floor, and out to the drop-off area. Cars come and go, but—as usual—Mom was right. It isn't that busy up here. I look for her blue Polo but don't see it, which means I'm alone with my thoughts for another few minutes.

Great. Now would be a good time for my mind to go blank.

Don't think about the guy who seems to no longer be your boyfriend.

Don't think about the guy you just kissed and will never see again.

Don't think about the sister you miss so much it makes you want to cry.

I open my handbag and pull out my book. I flip absentmindedly through it, trying to remember which page I was on. Reading is usually an excellent distraction, but the problem with *this* book is that I can no longer look at it without thinking of Aiden. I snap it shut as someone walks up to me.

I drop the book as my stomach falls through my toes and leaves my body entirely.

"Surprise!" says Matt.

7

SURPRISE?

What the ...

I don't ...

Is he *kidding* me?

Matt, looking perfectly groomed in a shirt and jeans, steps around the side of my trolley and gives me a peck on the cheek. He bends and picks up my fallen book, then says, "How was your flight?"

"I ... um ..." Maybe I'm dreaming. Maybe I'm still asleep on the plane and everything that's happened since we landed has been a ridiculous dream. "I ... I thought my mom was—"

"Oh, yeah, your mom and I thought it would be a nice surprise if I came to fetch you instead." Matt runs a hand through his neat, sandy coloured hair before pushing my trolley towards his car—which, it appears, managed to pull up in front of me without my noticing.

"I'm so confused right now," I mumble, but Matt doesn't seem to hear me as he loads my luggage into the boot. I get into the front passenger seat and put my seatbelt on, but still I don't wake up. I'm forced to face the horrifying fact that all of this is, indeed, happening.

"So tell me all about your holiday," Matt says as he turns his key in the ignition and pulls his car out of the parking space. I stare at him. We haven't exchanged a word since the night before I left, and now he's sitting next to me pretending it never happened? "Did you manage to get to all the places on your Top Tourist Destinations in London list?" he asks, seemingly oblivious to my state of shock and confusion.

Since there doesn't seem to be anything else to do, I haltingly tell Matt about the places Julia and I visited. Before long, he starts filling in my silent gaps with stories of his own visits to London, leaving me to watch the sugar cane fields rushing past and occasionally adding 'Uh huh' or 'Oh yeah, I saw that too' or some other appropriate comment.

As we turn off the highway and head through the streets that lead to my home, I imagine how different this drive would be if Aiden were beside me, seeing all of this for the first time. What would he think of the casino 'kingdom' in the middle of the sugar cane? What would he think of the minibus taxis blasting their music as they swerve around us and screech away at double the speed limit? Would he comment on how early the sun goes down compared to an English summer? The humidity? The *space*? And—as we turn into Girvan Avenue—what would he think of the fact that I live opposite an old, rundown cemetery? Would he think it's creepy? Cool? Not important at all? Would he be commenting on how large everyone's gardens are compared to the tiny backyards in London?

"… more books than I've ever seen in one place," Matt says at he parks in front of the gate to my house. "I knew you'd love it. You did go there, didn't you?"

"Hmm? Sorry?" I pull my gaze from the window and focus on Matt.

"Foyles. That giant bookstore in Charing Cross Road."

"Oh, yes. It was one of the first places Jules took me to."

The gate starts rolling open—Mom must have been on the lookout for us—as Matt jumps out the car and goes to the boot to fetch my luggage. I undo my seatbelt and climb out slowly. I breathe deeply and remind myself not to do anything weird, like start crying.

"Hey, are you feeling okay?" Matt asks. He slams the boot shut and wheels both suitcases to my side. "You've been very quiet. Did you get any sleep on the plane?"

"Uh, some." I rub my eyes and follow him up the driveway. "But, yeah, I'm quite tired."

Mom runs down the path from the front door, past Matt, and wraps me in a tight hug. "Welcome home!" she sings in my ear.

I hug her back and say, "You know I was only gone for three weeks, right?"

"Yes, yes," she steps back and examines me—for what? Could I really change that much in three weeks? "But you know I miss my chickens when they're not home." She gives me another quick hug, then pulls me up the path. "Aunt Maggie and Uncle Tom are coming for dinner, and I cooked Mexican. Your favourite. Will you be joining us, Matt?" she asks as we step through the front door to where Matt is leaning my suitcases against the wall.

"Oh, I'd love to, but I need to get home right away. We're heading to the farm just now. Spending the week there."

"Oh, that's lovely," Mom says. "But why are you leaving so late? Why not go tomorrow morning?"

Matt shrugs. "I don't know. My mom wants to. We were supposed to leave earlier today, but I told them I wanted to see Sarah before we left. Those three weeks without her were just *too* long." He pulls me into a sideways hug and kisses the top of my head while I try to wipe the look of confusion and I-just-tasted-something-bad off my face.

"Sarah! My favourite middle daughter!" Dad calls from the lounge before striding into the entrance hall and greeting me with a hug. "I hope you videoed your entire visit to the Science Museum."

I pull out of the hug and say, "Darn, I knew I forgot something." At the look of disappointment on his face, I quickly add, "Relax, Dad. Jules and I did at least five mini interviews at various places inside the museum. She was more than happy to stand in front of my phone and act all goofy while talking about science.

"Anyway," I continue, "Matt needs to go now, so I'm gonna say goodbye, and then I'll tell you all about it."

My parents take the hint and disappear into the lounge to give me a moment alone with Matt. I turn to him, and I'm about to ask what's going on between us, but he takes my face in both hands and presses his mouth against mine before I can get a word out. He tastes of familiarity and … guilt. Because the last person I kissed wasn't him. I try to relax against him and remember all the butterflies and goosebumps I used to get when he kissed me, but he's already pulling away. "I missed you," he says, then adds a quick kiss to my nose. "And now I've gotta go."

I clench my fists at my sides as he turns away. *SAY SOMETHING!* "Matt, I'm … I'm a little confused. The night before I left …"

"Yes," he says, stopping and turning back. "Yes, I know." He looks down. "We were both angry. We both said very hurtful things we ended up regretting, and … well, now that we've had a few weeks to cool off, I think we should just put it behind us, you know?" He raises his eyes to mine and gives me an encouraging smile. "All couples fight. It's normal. There's no reason we can't get back to the way things used to be between us." He tucks my hair behind my ear. "We're good together, Sarah. I'd hate to lose what we have."

He gives me one last hug, and I mumble, "O-okay," because somehow it doesn't feel like he left much else for me to say.

"Anyway, I need to go. I'll see you on Friday morning." He ducks out the front door and heads down the path while I try to figure out what he's talking about.

"Friday morning?" I call after him.

"Yeah, I'm coming back to pick you up to take you to the farm." He looks over his shoulder and, at the blank look on my face, rolls his eyes. "Grandpa's ninetieth, remember? The party's next weekend? I told you about it months ago."

"Uh, yeah." I do remember, but for some reason I'd thought it was happening after Christmas. "Okay, see you then." I lean inside and press the button to close the gate. When I look back out, Sophie is running up the driveway.

"Hello, *sis*!" she shouts, then just about collides into me. I wrap my arms around my younger sister, and we do a kind of bouncy hug thing that starts us both giggling.

"Where'd you just come from?" I ask her once we've recovered from our laughter.

"I was down the road at Braden's."

I raise my hands to make quote marks in the air. "You mean 'that boy'?"

Sophie groans and closes the front door. "Yeah, Mom still doesn't like him much."

She helps me carry my luggage down the passage to my bedroom, where I see a brown paper bag sitting on the bed. I open the bag and look inside. "Biltong! Fantastic!" I stick my hand in and remove a few pieces of the finely sliced dried meat. "I've been craving biltong the whole time I was away."

"I know," says Sophie. "You mentioned it on Facebook, so I told Mom."

I munch on the salty, spicy snack and mumble, "You rock."

Sophie smiles sweetly and says again, "I know." She pushes her blonde hair over her shoulder, then holds her hand out, palm up.

Jules and I both have dark hair like our parents, but somehow Sophie wound up blonde. She used to get upset about it when she was little—'Why don't I look like the rest of you?'—and Jules would tell her every time that she'd always secretly wished she had Sophie's beautiful golden locks. That would inevitably lead to Sophie begging someone to tell her the story of *Goldilocks and the Three Bears*, and by the time that was finished, she'd always forgotten she was upset in the first place.

I shake the paper bag over Sophie's hand until several pieces of biltong fall out. "So *that's* why you told Mom about my craving," I say. "You knew you'd score some for yourself."

Sophie smiles but doesn't say anything.

"Hey, hey, hey," Mom says, appearing suddenly in the doorway. "Don't fill up on biltong. We're having dinner soon. Aunt Maggie and Uncle Tom are almost here."

She hurries away—probably back to the kitchen—and Sophie puts a few more pieces into her mouth. The sneaky look on her face reminds me of Julia, which sends an unhappy lurch through me, which then gets me thinking about Aiden, which, in turn, twists my insides further.

I push the thought of either of them from my mind. "Want to see all the cool stuff I got overseas?" I say to Sophie.

"Yes, definitely." She sits cross-legged on my bed while I

unzip my suitcase, and even though I've never really connected with my younger sister the way I have with Julia, I'm so glad to have her right now.

When Aunt Maggie and Uncle Tom have left, and everyone else has gone to bed, I find myself alone in my bedroom. The excitement of photographs and travel stories and handing out all the gifts I bought has passed. Julia's absence and Aiden's absence and the inevitability of having to return to a university degree I don't even like after Christmas settle over me like one of those heavy apron things they cover you with when you have an X-ray at the dentist.

I finish unpacking my clothes, throwing most of them into a pile near the door to wash in the morning. When I get to the bottom of my carry-on suitcase, I slowly remove my notebook. I stand up and rub my thumb over the shiny, paisley-patterned cover. I flip through it—pages and pages of scribbled words squished close together—before opening the bottom drawer of my desk and tossing the notebook inside. I gather the rest of my notebooks from my bookshelf and add them to the drawer, then slam it shut. I don't want to see inside those notebooks again. I don't want to read my amateurish scribbles. They almost caused me to miss a flight, and—far worse—they caused all the hurtful things Matt and I said to each other the night before I left.

When I've finished unpacking and changed into

pyjamas—summer pyjamas! No more climbing into bed covered in at least four different layers!—I open the lid of my ancient laptop and turn it on. I wait patiently while the aged beast grumbles, whirs, and blows hot air in its attempt to start up. After several minutes, it seems to be alive and ready. I open the browser and head to Facebook. I scroll through the news feed for a few minutes, but no matter how many videos of cute toddler relatives or captioned pictures of weird cats or random status updates I see, I can't stop my eyes from continually moving up to the search bar at the top of the page.

Aiden. I want to search for Aiden. The problem is, I don't know his surname. I caught a glimpse of the name tag on his luggage, but all I remember is that his surname ends in *ison*. I think. Which doesn't exactly help.

Maybe it's better that I don't know his full name. After all, it feels like it might be wrong to search for him. Like in some weird way I'm cheating on Matt.

Okay, look, I tell myself. *You thought you and Matt were no longer together when you kissed Aiden, so you didn't really do anything wrong there. And he technically kissed you, not the other way around. And all you want now is to be friends with him. Nothing wrong with looking him up on Facebook just for that.*

I open a new tab and go to Google. I hesitate, my fingers hovering over the keyboard.

"What are you doing?" I whisper to myself.

Before I can change my mind, I type *surnames ending in "ison"* into the search bar. I scan the results that come up, but I don't see anything too helpful. I was hoping for a list or something. I look at a few articles and pick out some surnames—Addison, Morrison, Bettison, Madison—before returning to Facebook. I try each surname paired with the name Aiden, but I don't find the guy I'm looking for.

"It's just not meant to be," I mutter to myself. I close the laptop with a mixture of disappointment and relief settling in my stomach. I climb into bed with my phone—which is about a century ahead of my laptop in terms of technology—and open the email app. I saw an email from Livi when I was scrolling through messages at the airport, and I think I could do with some best friend love right now. I smile at the words in the subject line: **You smell nice**. Livi likes to title her emails with weird statements that have nothing to do with the content, just to make sure nobody misses them. I'm amazed half the messages I've received from her haven't ended up in the Spam folder.

I tap the screen to open her email.

From: Alivia Howard <livi-gem@gmail.com>
Sent: Sat 14 Dec, 8:13 pm
To: Sarah Henley <s.henley@gmail.com>
Subject: You smell nice

One week and counting! Woohoo! I am SO glad this year is almost over—I never want to see another German brat in my life. And BOY do I have a story to tell you! A story involving a BOY, actually ;-) I don't think even your made-up stories can top this one! We need to book a poolside date SOON so I can tell you all about it.

xx Livi

From: Sarah Henley <s.henley@gmail.com>
Sent: Sun 15 Dec, 10:34 pm
To: Alivia Howard <livi-gem@gmail.com>
Subject: Re: You smell nice

Oh, I think I have a story that might top yours. And mine isn't made up either!

From: Sarah Henley <s.henley@gmail.com>
Sent: Sun 15 Dec, 10:37 pm
To: Julia Henley <info@lumenography.co>
Subject: Never again shall you mock the travel toothbrush

Jules! You will never guess what happened to me on the plane ...

HARRISON!

I wake up on Friday morning with the name on the tip of my tongue, and I'm convinced it belongs to Aiden. I know I caught a glimpse of the label on his bag, and when I close my eyes, I can clearly see an 'H' after his first name. I guess my brain just needed a few days to remember that detail—or it could be that after a few days of obsessing, my brain manufactured a false memory while I was sleeping.

To prove to myself that I *haven't* been obsessing over Aiden, and that I *don't* care whether I've remembered his surname correctly or not, I intentionally bypass my laptop on the way to the shower. It already feels about five hundred degrees hotter than any day should ever have the right to be at 8 am, so I turn the shower tap until the water is as cold as it will go. Afterwards, I take my time choosing a pretty summer dress. I eat breakfast slowly, make my bed, and start packing my bag for a weekend at Matt's grandparents' farm—all while pretending half my brain *isn't* focused on the laptop in the corner of my room, as if it has some magnetic influence over my thoughts. I choose a pair of shorts, another dress, some summer pyjamas that are appropriate to wear in front of other people—*not* my old-enough-to-be-transparent nightie with the cartoon cow and *Over the moooooooon* written on it—and then try to remember which of my three bikinis Matt likes the most. Because I'm supposed to be thinking of him, not Aiden. Matt is my boyfriend. Matt is the guy who loves me. Matt is the one I'll probably spend the rest of my—

"Oh, this is ridiculous." I drop the tangle of bikinis onto my bed and rush to the corner of my room. I sit down at the desk and open the lid of my laptop. The machine whirs for a moment or two, then blinks out of hibernation mode and shows the last page I was on: my email. I open a new tab and navigate to Facebook. The moment the site loads, I type 'Aiden Harrison' into the search bar. A second passes, and then a whole list of Aiden Harrisons show up. I lean forward, examining the tiny profile picture next to each name. *Not him ... not him ... not him ... not him ... Is that ... ?* My heart does an uncomfortable double beat thing and a tiny squeal escapes my throat as I recognise the fifth Aiden Harrison.

It's him! I've found him!

Okay. Breathe. Calm down. I push my wheeled chair away from the desk and pat out a random rhythm across my knees. What am I doing? Am I going to send him a friend request? And then what? What if he accepts? What if he doesn't? What if he's not using his phone or a computer or anything while he's on holiday and he only sees the friend request when he gets home and doesn't even remember who I am?

But he is using his phone, I remind myself. I remember returning to the Häagen-Dazs table in Dubai airport with two cups of ice cream in my hands and seeing him frown at it as though he didn't like what he saw there.

Okay, one step at a time. I reach for the edge of the desk and pull myself back towards it. I'll check out his profile—whatever I can see without actually being his friend—and then decide. Ignoring the fact this probably makes me an instant stalker, I click on his name.

Once his page has loaded, I can see his profile picture in more detail. He's smiling and looking at something outside the frame of the photo, and in the background colourful houses sprout from a mountainside that ends with a sheer drop into a blue, blue sea. Scrolling down his page reveals the photos he's used as profile pictures in the past—some group shots, a few arbitrary pictures that don't include him at all, and several with his arm around a pretty dark-haired girl. The most recent photo with her is dated eight months ago, though, so I'm hoping that means he isn't with her anymore. Not that I have any right to hope for things like that, considering I still have a boyfriend.

I scroll back up to the top of the page and stare at the 'Add Friend' button. I move my mouse over it but don't click it. I try to figure out what I want from Aiden. It can't be more than friendship, of course, since he'll be returning to England soon—and there's Matt. A guy I *want* to be with. Because people don't just throw away two-year relationships for random guys they met on a plane and *think* they had some connection with. So … I'll click the button, wait for him to accept the friendship request, then tell him that even though I really enjoyed the kiss, I actually have a boyfriend and—no, wait, I *won't* tell him I enjoyed the kiss. I'll just say that I have a boyfriend, but I'd like to still be friends with Aiden. Because I enjoyed chatting to him. And it felt like we connected on some level. Or whatever. I'll figure it out when he responds.

I tap my finger absently on the edge of my laptop and continue staring at the button. I stare at it for so long that I don't realise how much time has passed until the gate buzzer sounds and Sophie shouts, "Matt's here!"

My head jerks towards the open doorway of my bedroom, as if Matt might already be standing there watching what I'm doing. I turn back to the screen and the 'Add Friend' button. I clench my fists over the keyboard.

Come on, just make a decision. Make a decision.

I hit the button, then jump up and back away from the computer as if it might bite me.

"Hey, Soph," Matt says from the entrance hall. "How's it going?"

I dart forward and slam the lid of my laptop shut.

It's done. Stop thinking about it now. Finish packing your bag.

Matt appears in my doorway just as I shove all three bikinis into my suitcase. I'm normally a much neater packer, but I don't exactly have time right now. "Hey," Matt says. He crosses the room and gives me a quick hug and a kiss. "You almost ready?"

"Yeah, just give me a few more minutes." I grab a book from my bedside table and slide it carefully into the top pocket of my suitcase. I might be happy shoving certain things into my bag, but books are not one of them.

"Babe, come on," Matt says. "I sent you a message when I left, and it took me, like, three hours to get here. I thought you'd be packed by now."

"Yeah, I know. I got side-tracked. But I'm almost finished, I promise." I duck past him and hurry to the bathroom to pack my toiletries.

Ten minutes later, I've said goodbye to my family and am wheeling my small suitcase—the same one I used for carry-on luggage—towards Matt's car. He lifts it into the back seat, closes the door, and looks at me as if noticing something for the first time. "You look pretty," he says. "Not as pale as when I saw you on Sunday. Did you spend some time in the sun this week?"

"Yes. I managed to get quite a bit of tanning done, actually."

"Cool. I hope you brought nicer shoes, though," he adds as he stares pointedly at my slip-slops. "You need to look a little smarter for the party this afternoon."

"Of course," I say with a sigh as I open the passenger door. "They're in my suitcase."

Matt likes to talk a lot, which works out well for us, since I'd rather be listening than talking. He spends the first half hour of our drive to the Drakensberg telling me about the game of golf he played with his dad yesterday. I try to remain interested, but I've always found golf to be a particularly boring game—perhaps not too boring if I were on the golf course witnessing a game myself, but certainly boring enough when I'm being given a blow-by-blow second-hand account of every blade of grass.

I pull my phone out of my bag, open the Facebook app, check whether there's a response from Aiden yet—there isn't—and then feel so guilty that I'm sitting next to my boyfriend while looking for a message from another guy that I log out of the app immediately and decide not to log back in for the rest of the weekend.

I watch Matt while he continues chatting. Most girls find him attractive, but I think it has more to do with his confidence and his winning smile than his actual physical features—although there's nothing wrong with those. He seems at ease now, the way he always does, one elbow leaning against the window while his hand loosely grips the steering wheel. His other hand rests on my knee.

For weeks after we started dating, I'd catch myself staring at him and thinking, *I can't believe he picked* me! This good-looking, friendly, everything-he-touches-works-out-in-his-favour guy picked *me* to be his girlfriend. He must have been aware of my epic shyness, because weeks passed between the moment he first showed interest in me and the day he finally asked me out. Weeks of shy smiles, notes passed in class, awkward conversations in corridors, and rumours that he liked me. By the time he asked me out, I was convinced I was already in love with him. I was convinced I'd never love anyone else the way I loved him.

But now ... now I can't help wondering something. If Matt had never shown any interest in me, would I ever have wanted to be with him? Would I have liked him simply for being *him*, or was it only because he liked me first?

"Why did you ask me out?" The words have left my mouth before I can stop them. Before I can even *think* them. It's as if my mouth has taken over and left my brain behind.

Looking as startled as I feel, Matt says, "What?"

"I ... I mean ... what first attracted you to me? Why were you interested in me? We didn't run in the same social circles back at school, so ... I mean, you didn't know me at all."

"Uh ..." Matt is one of those guys who usually has an immediate answer for everything—even if it's an answer that's rubbish—so his hesitation surprises me. He looks straight ahead at the road, both hands on the wheel now, and says, "I think the first time I noticed you was during that English book review oral we had to do at the beginning of matric. I'd only ever known you as That Really Shy Girl." He looks at me then, his confident smile back in place, and adds, "That Really *Pretty* Shy Girl," and I can't help smiling with him. "I don't think I'd ever heard you speak before," he continues, "so that was the first thing that interested me. The next thing was when you started talking. I could tell you were nervous, but you were so passionate about the book you were reviewing, that the nerves didn't show that much. I have no idea what book it was, but I remember that you spoke so intelligently, so *intensely*, that it was as if you understood that book better than anyone else who'd ever read it. And right then, I thought, 'I want to know more about this girl.'"

I start blushing and look down at my lap. "I love you," I say quietly.

He grips my knee again. "I love you too, babe."

He turns the radio up and sings along while I watch the towns slipping away on either side of us. The mountains come into view slowly, first as a hazy blue-grey line of bumps in the distance, then taking shape and growing in size as we get closer. By the time we turn off the tar and onto the tree-lined dirt road that leads to Matt's grandparents' farm, the mountains are all around us, their peaks looking deceptively close.

We drive through an open gate, beside which stands a wooden pole with an aged sign nailed to the top of it: Millers' Place.

We've arrived.

THE ROAD LEADING UP TO THE OLD FARMHOUSE IS ALWAYS longer than I remember. On the left, the trees are too numerous to see between, but on the right, I catch glimpses of the lake and the hills and mountains rising beyond it.

"You'll be sharing a room with Simone and Elize," Matt tells me.

"Oh. Okay." Matt's Afrikaans cousins aren't my favourite people in the world, but I can deal with them for three nights. "There must be quite a few people coming if three of us have to stay in one room," I add, thinking of the many bedrooms and bathrooms I came across while exploring the farmhouse in previous visits.

"Well, you know how big my family is. Some of them are staying in a resort nearby, but everyone else has descended upon Nan and Grandpa hoping for free accommodation."

"I bet Nan loves it, though."

"I think Grandpa loves it even more."

I smile to myself. Of all the people in Matt's extensive family, I think I like Grandpa the most. After I got to know him, I admitted one day that my brain always seems to be making up stories. He looked at me as though there were no one else in the world he'd rather be listening to and said, "Tell me one of your stories." And so, going completely against my character, I did.

The road bends to the left, and the farmhouse comes into view. Gravel crunches beneath the tires as Matt steers his car around to the back where a long awning is already providing shelter for at least ten cars.

Uneasiness stirs inside me. "So, um, is everyone else here already?"

Matt's eyes flick to the time on the dashboard: 3:38 pm. "Probably not, since the party only officially starts at four." He squeezes his car into the only space left beneath the awning. "Everyone who's staying here started arriving this morning, so I guess they're around somewhere, but I don't know about all the people from the resort."

I unbuckle my seatbelt and open my door. "It must have been nice to have a quiet week here with just your grandparents before the hordes started arriving."

"Well, it was hardly a relaxing holiday." Matt removes my suitcase from the back of the car. "You know my mom practically organised this entire thing herself, so every day she was issuing orders to the rest of us to get stuff done."

I stare up at the house while Matt locks his car. "I didn't realise it was such a big thing," I say quietly.

"He's turning ninety, Sarah. It might be the last party the old man gets."

"Matt!"

"What? It's the truth."

Matt takes my hand and I walk with him past the cars to the open back door. I can hear the bustle of activity coming from the kitchen as we approach it. "I told you not to pinch!" someone says. I step inside in time to see a small, squealing girl dashing out the door on the opposite side of the kitchen, followed closely by Nan.

"I'm going to catch you!"

"Oh, you're back," Matt's mother says, hurrying towards us in an apron. "Sarah, it's lovely to see you." She gives me a quick half-hug, then leans around me to grab a cloth hanging on the back of the door. She rushes back to the other side of the kitchen, where platters of food are lined up across the counter, and wipes at something I can't see.

"We should probably get out of the way," Matt says to me. I wave a quick hello to Josephine and Zukie, the two domestic ladies who help Nan in the house, then follow Matt out of the kitchen. He leads the way up a creaky wooden staircase and along a carpeted passage to a bedroom with two single beds and a blow-up mattress. A pair of sunglasses and a flowery backpack sit on one bed, while an iPod and some rumpled clothes lie across the other.

"I guess you're taking the mattress," Matt says.

"Yeah."

"I'll see you downstairs when you're ready." He leaves

my suitcase next to the other two on the floor and heads back down the passage.

I kick off my slip-slops and unzip the suitcase. My blue wedges are the only 'smart' shoes I brought, so they'll just have to be smart enough for Matt. I sit on the floor while I tie the straps around my ankles, then search my toiletry bag for the earrings I threw in just before leaving home. I put them on, then unclip my hair and let it fall down my back and over my shoulders. I had plans to straighten my hair into a smooth, sleek version of itself this morning, but after staring at the 'Add Friend' button for so long, I ran out of time. So I'm going with the naturally wavy look. Again, probably not what Matt had in mind for me when he said 'smart,' but I think I look fine. I stand, smooth my hands over my dress, and head downstairs.

The lawn in front of the farmhouse looks like a page out of a wedding magazine. Fairy lights are strung from the trees, and jars with candles in them hang here and there. Numerous round tables are covered in white cloths, flower arrangements, and silver photo frames—which I know, from having seen them lined up at Matt's house, each contain a different photo of Grandpa with family members and friends. The whole area is outlined by a collection of shepherd's crooks, each with a jar of flowers hanging from it, and overhead, strings of pale blue and white bunting criss-cross from the highest tree branches to the windows of some of the upstairs bedrooms.

My first thought is that if I end up marrying Matt, I'll be happy to let his mother take full control of the decor. My second thought is that the idea of marrying Matt makes me feel anxious instead of excited. And my third thought is that there are *far* more people out here than I'm comfortable with. I'm about to back away into the house when Matt comes to my rescue. He jogs up the two steps onto the veranda and comes to my side.

"Shall I get you a drink?" he asks. Before waiting for my answer, he squeezes between people to the other end of the veranda where a long table is covered with rows of glasses. He speaks to the guy standing behind the table, then returns and hands me a champagne glass with peach-coloured liquid and floating bits of fruit.

I take a sip while Matt starts chatting to an old man standing next to us. Matt knows I have a tendency to go blank in front of strangers, so he doesn't expect me to do much more than smile sweetly and answer any questions that might come my way. As their conversation turns to sport—something Matt has never expected me to comment on—I look around and attempt to organise Matt's extended family in my head. Grandpa is Matt's mother's father, so everyone here will be from her side of the family. There's Uncle Number One, who married an Afrikaans girl and produced Elize and Simone, my roommates for the weekend; Uncle Number Two, who married later in life and has an adorable two-year-old who's currently toddling around on the grass entertaining a small audience; and an aunt I've never met who may or may not be here. Then there are various cousins of Matt's mother's generation—Grandpa's nieces and nephews—and some of their offspring, but that's where I start getting completely lost. And since I don't plan on speaking to most of them, it doesn't really matter.

"Sarah was actually just over there," Matt says, nudging my arm to get my attention.

"Oh really?" The-man-whose-name-I-don't-know looks at me. "Dreadful weather they're having over there at the moment. I heard they might have to close Heathrow."

"Oh?" I try to look interested. "I hadn't heard that."

"That would certainly be—oh, Sarah, you haven't met my Aunt Hannah yet, have you?" Matt nods a goodbye to the old man, then steers me towards a woman who looks like a lighter-haired version of his mother. "Aunt Hannah, this is my girlfriend, Sarah. Sarah, this is the aunt who's been dreadful enough not to visit us since I was about five years old." Matt laughs, and Aunt Hannah laughs, and I add in a chuckle even though right now all I want to do is hide in the kitchen with Josephine and Zukie. "And she brought my cousins with as well," Matt adds. He looks around, then points to a girl sitting at one of the round tables on the grass talking to Grandpa—Grandpa! Whom I haven't greeted or wished happy birthday to yet! "That's Emily. And … oh, here he is." Matt steps aside. "This is my other overseas cousin, Aiden."

My hand clenches around my champagne glass. I look up.

Tall. Dark, somewhat messy hair. Blue-green eyes.

Smash!

"Oh!" I step back automatically as my glass hits the stone

tiles of the veranda. "I—I'm so sorry."

"Sarah," Matt groans.

"I'm so sorry." I take another step back, looking all around me, everywhere except at *him*. "I—I'll get that cleaned up." I duck behind Matt, squeeze past another group of people, and rush into the house. I run to the kitchen as fast as my wedges will carry me. I dart inside and press my back against the fridge.

No! What is Aiden doing here? WHAT IS HE DOING HERE?

"Sarah?" I look up and see Josephine with a jug of water in one hand and an empty plastic bottle in the other. "What's wrong?"

"I … um … nothing. I mean, yes, I dropped a glass and it broke." I step away from the fridge and look wildly around. "Where … I just need a dustpan. If you could show me where—"

"I'll do it, don't worry." Zukie steps away from the sink and dries her hands on the dish towel hanging over her shoulder.

"No, no, no. I'll do it. I'm the one who made the mess. Just show me where—"

Zukie laughs and waves me out of her way. "Relax. They pay me to clean up, remember?" She removes a dustpan and brush from a cupboard and disappears.

"Are you sure you're all right?" Josephine asks, narrowing her eyes at me.

"I, uh, yes. I'll just be … out there." I point to the back

door, then hurry through it. I squeeze past the cars to where the awning ends and lean my back against the wall. I stare up at the mountains. *Okay, seriously?* I say to God. *You know I wanted to see him again, but why does he have to show up* here? *Why does he have to be Matt's* cousin? *Is this some kind of punishment for obsessing over a guy who isn't my boyfriend?*

I wish the mountains would speak back to me, but I get nothing. Nothing but the assurance that I could fling my questions at them today, tomorrow, or in a hundred years, and they would still be there. Ever-present and never changing.

I head slowly back to the kitchen, wondering if anyone will miss me if I hide there until it's time to sit down for dinner. I step through the doorway and see a white-haired figure bending over one of the platters on the counter and saying, "I'm sure no one will miss this particular pie. This plate is looking a little crowded anyway."

"Go right ahead, sir," Zukie says. "It's your party, after all."

"Grandpa!" I say. He turns around with the guilty expression of a child caught pinching cookies. I start laughing as I cross the kitchen. "Happy birthday, Grandpa." I put my arms around him and squeeze, remembering the very first time I hugged him. I was so aware of how frail he seemed that I barely touched him at all. He said, 'Now, that's a sad excuse for a hug. You can do better than that.'

"Sarah, dear, how lovely of you to join us." He returns the squeeze and pats my back.

"What are you doing in here?" I ask when I step back. "Aren't there about a hundred people out there who want to speak to you?"

"More, probably," Granpda says with a wink. "I was just catching a few minutes of quiet before moving onto the next family member." He leans over and lifts a mini pie from the platter. "And grabbing a snack. No one will give me a minute to eat anything out there." He takes a bite and chews.

"Any good?" I ask.

"Mmm." He swallows. "Exceptional. Well, I suppose my break is over. I'll find you again later so you can tell me what happens next in that exciting robot story of yours." He pats my shoulder, then heads out of the kitchen.

I wait a few moments, then decide it's time to face the two boys I can't exactly hide from the whole weekend. After all, I've been wishing I could see Aiden again, and now here he is. Even if I'm too terrified to talk to him—because surely he knows by now that the guy who just introduced the two of us is my boyfriend—I can at least look at him. Or not. Because staring at my boyfriend's hot cousin probably isn't what I want to be caught doing at a family reunion. I can just imagine the rumours that would start flying around. Rumours that would no doubt reach Matt's ears before dinner even begins.

I take slow steps out of the kitchen, down the passage, and across the lounge. Instead of going out onto the veranda, I stand at the window and look out. My eyes skim across the groups of chatting people, but I don't see Aiden anywhere. Perhaps he—

"Hiding in the bathroom again?"

I jump at the familiar voice behind me, and if I'd been holding another glass, I probably would have dropped it. I twist my head around and see Aiden walking towards me. "I, uh—"

"You seem to have a habit of doing that," he says.

I look down at the floor. "No, I wasn't, actually."

I watch his feet as he moves to stand beside me, but when I raise my eyes, he's staring resolutely out of the window. "Twenty hours," he says. "Twenty hours talking about everything from parallel dimensions to how you feel mediocre compared to your sisters, and you didn't once think to mention that you have a *boyfriend*?"

"I … I didn't know …"

"You didn't know what, Sarah? That you have a boyfriend?" He turns to face me then, waiting for me to say something, but I can't squeeze a sound out. "That is the most ridiculous thing I've ever heard. Matt says the two of you have been dating for almost two years. How could you *not know* that that means you have a boyfriend?"

"I know that's what it means," I mumble. "It's just that we—"

"I *kissed* you! I never would have done that if I'd known you were with someone."

Why did you kiss me? I want to ask, but instead I stammer, "I … it's complicated—"

"Oh, of course. Everything's always complicated, isn't it?" He shakes his head as he looks out the window once more.

"Can you just let me explain what I mean? You don't understand—"

"I don't think there's much to *understand* other than the fact that you led me to believe something that isn't true."

"I—what do you—when did I—"

"Just forget it," he says, turning towards the door without another glance in my direction. Before stepping onto the veranda, he looks back. "Did you finish reading that book?" he asks, but it's less of a question and more of an accusation. Like I wasted his time by making him hurry back into the airport to give it to him. Like somehow I tricked him into kissing me.

I clench my hands into fists at my sides. "Yes," I lie. "And it finished exactly the way I predicted." I push past him and cross the veranda as quickly as I can, my anger already coalescing into hot tears behind my eyes. I blink them away as I slip past people.

Find your table. Sit down. Don't make eye contact with anyone.

After examining the name tags on several of the round tables, I eventually find mine next to Matt's. On the other side of Matt's place, nineteen-year-old Elize and her younger sister are already sitting down. They're leaning over a cell phone, giggling like little girls. I've spoken to the two of them enough times not to freak out about opening my mouth in front of them, so I mumble hello as I slide into my chair.

They look up, greet me, and then Elize straightens and

points to someone. *"O, daar is hy!"* she says to Simone. *"Die hot ou wat ek jou van vertel het. Hy's myne."* I pull my chair closer to the table and follow Elize's line of sight to see this 'hot guy' she's already claimed.

Aiden. Of course. Who else would she be pointing at?

"Is ons nie familie van hom nie?" Simone asks.

Well done, Simone, I almost say. *You are indeed related to him.*

"Nee." Elize giggles. *"Ek sou definitief geweet het as ons familie was van daai ou."*

Simone scrunches her nose up in confusion. *"Ek dog ons is familie van almal hier."*

I roll my eyes. "His name is Aiden. I'm pretty sure he's your cousin."

Elize's mouth drops open. "That's *Aiden? Tannie* Hannah's son?" She tilts her head to the side as she examines him. "But I thought everyone from England was pale with bad teeth." She slumps across the table and groans, then lifts her head and turns back to the cell phone. *"Ag toemaar,"* she says to Simone. *"Ek kan hom in elk geval nie hê nie."*

"Ek het jou mos gesê," Simone mutters.

I look around the table and try to make out the other name tags. Next to me I've got Matt's older sister and her boyfriend, and next to them—I lean over to read the swirly writing on the little pieces of card—Matt's older brother and his girlfriend.

I sit back in my chair with some relief. At least I don't have to live through the awkwardness of both Aiden and Matt sitting at the same table as me all night. But half an hour later, when Matt's mother starts ushering everyone towards their seats and Aiden crosses the lawn and comes straight towards me, I realise tonight's awkwardness is far from over. Not only is he at the table adjacent to ours, but he's sitting in the chair right behind me.

From: Facebook
<notification+oo425304@facebookmail.com>
Sent: Fri 20 Dec, 11:51 pm
To: Sarah Henley <s.henley@gmail.com>
Subject: New message from Aiden Harrison

I'm sorry about earlier. I had no right to be upset with you. How about we pretend everything since that last moment at the airport didn't happen and start over? Still want to be friends?

Sent from Facebook. Reply to this email to message Aiden Harrison.

I'm lying on my mattress early on Saturday morning looking through messages from the night before when I come across the Facebook message from Aiden. I read it, close my eyes, and cringe at the memory of the previous night. Matt putting his arm around me, kissing my neck, making loud jokes—all with Aiden sitting not half a metre behind us.

I quickly type a reply (Yes, please. I'm sorry too.), then place my phone on the floor. I wonder if Aiden's awake now. Is he waiting for my reply? I was hoping his family might be staying at the resort nearby, but no. Down the passage and around the corner is the room Aiden is sharing with—guess who?—Matt and his brother.

I turn onto my back and stare at the ceiling. *Still want to be friends?* There are a great many areas in my life where I don't know what I want, but I know I want Aiden as a friend. A tiny part of me wants more than that, but mostly I just want what we had on the plane. Honest conversation. A connection. The feeling that someone understands me and doesn't think I'm a total fruit loop.

I sit up and look across the room. Elize and Simone are both still asleep. Elize's hair—the topmost layers dyed white-blonde, and the underneath layers dyed black—is fanned out across her pillow. Simone is snuggled so far beneath her duvet, I can only just see the top of her dark brown head. I'd love to turn over and do exactly the same thing, but since the ratio of people to bathrooms is about five to one, I should probably take my chance while there's still hot water and no queue.

I quietly gather up my toiletries, towel, and some clothes, and tiptoe out of the room. My bare feet make no noise on the carpeted floor as I head towards the bathroom. I see the open door, and I let out a silent *Yes!* at the fact that I won't have to wait for anyone. But as I reach the doorway, someone turns the corner at the end of the passage and almost walks right into me.

"Whoa, sorry," Aiden says, running a hand through his messy hair. He blinks, and from the look on his face, I'm pretty sure he woke up about ten seconds ago.

"Um, you can go," I say quickly, stepping back.

"What? No, you're all ready and … stuff." He gestures to the collection of belongings in my arms, which I hug against my chest. I'm somewhat decently clothed in sleep shorts and a T-shirt, but still. No bra. I hug my bundle closer.

"It's fine," I say. "I mean, you're gonna be quick, aren't you? You're just gonna …" Oh hell, why am I making reference to what he may or may not be doing in the bathroom? Just SHUT UP, Sarah!

"It's cool," Aiden says, raising his hands and stepping past me. "I'll find another one. You can use this one."

I step inside, close the door, and groan as I slump against it. Why do I have to embarrass myself every time I open my mouth? I fling my towel over the side of the shower and undress. I'm about to turn on the water when a bang on the door startles me. "Hurry up in there," Elize calls. "There's a queue."

Matt suggested last night that we go for a hike today, an idea I was excited about until Aiden turned out to be one of the other eight people who also thought it was a great idea. As much as I want to spend time with him, it's weird when Matt is also around. It's as if the me Matt knows is a little different from the me Aiden knows, and I'm not sure how to be both of them at the same time.

I sit on one of the couches in the lounge downstairs after lunch, lacing up my shoes while Elize plaits Simone's hair and Emily covers every inch of her pale skin with sunscreen. I haven't had a chance to speak to Aiden's older sister—which means I'd probably stutter something unintelligible if she started talking to me now—but from the snippets of conversation I overheard last night and this morning, she seems like a nice person. Probably the kind of person I could be friends with if I were brave enough to get over my debilitating shyness.

"How intense is this hike?" she asks, her words as accented as Aiden's. "Do any of you know? I'm a bit worried I'll slow everyone down."

"I'm sure you'll manage just fine," Aiden says as he walks into the lounge. He removes his sunglasses—when have sunglasses *ever* looked so sexy?—and sits beside his sister. "Matt said it's about four hours in total, with some steep bits here and there, but nothing too hectic. I'm sure your long legs can make it to the top and back just as easily as anyone else."

Emily gives Aiden a friendly punch on the arm. "Not all of us have just come back from a walking holiday. We can't all be as fit as you."

"So, Emily, I heard you're getting married soon," Elize

says as she winds a hairband around the end of Simon's plait. "That's cool. First wedding for your family. I'm hoping I'll beat Simone, but you never know what might happen."

Across the room, Aiden looks away and shifts slightly on the couch, and I wonder if he has something against Emily's fiancé. Emily's eyes flick towards her brother for a moment, but then she looks at Elize. "Yes, it's incredibly exciting," she says as a smile that obviously can't be suppressed spreads across her face. "I'm soon to be Mrs Winterbottom."

Simone scrunches up her face and says, "Really? You sure you want to be a *Winterbottom* for the rest of your life?"

Emily smiles. "I know, I know, it's not the nicest surname, but ... I love him, so it's a sacrifice I'm happy to make."

"Your poor children," Elize says with a sigh. "My best friend since, like, forever has suffered from an embarrassing surname her entire life, so I know how mean kids can be about weird names."

"Was it really that bad?" Emily asks. "What's her surname?"

"Haasbroek."

"Oh." Emily's face is politely blank. Aiden looks at me and raises an eyebrow.

"Bunnypants," I supply.

"*Oh*," Emily says, then covers her mouth as she starts laughing.

Matt jogs into the lounge and stops beside the couch I'm

sitting on. "Okay, so two people have bailed to join the easy walk all the adults are doing, so we're just waiting for Malcolm and Aunt Hannah, and then we can go."

Half an hour later, when Matt's older brother Malcolm and Aunt Hannah have joined us, we head along the path that rings the lake. On the other side, we climb through trees towards the foot of the mountain where the hike starts. Matt and Malcolm talk about the future of Malcolm's start-up business, Emily and her mother discuss wedding details, Elize tosses her hair about and hangs onto every word Aiden says, and Simone and I find ourselves with no one to talk to.

The first hour drags by as we climb rocks and follow sandy paths, always looking out for the next blue arrow painted onto a rock or wooden stump to point the way. The arrows have survived years of varying weather conditions, but some have almost faded completely. Matt's eyes are sharp, though, and he never misses an arrow.

After listening to Elize's giggle for far too long, Aiden manages to convince her to ask Emily about her wedding plans. As Elize takes her sister's hand and hurries forward to catch up to Emily, Aiden slows until he's walking beside me.

"Enjoying your hike?" I ask him, wiping the back of my hand across my sweaty brow.

"More than I was a moment ago," he says, his voice low enough not to carry forwards. "How about you?"

"It was getting a little lonely back here, but I love the mountains no matter who's keeping me company."

"Really?" Aiden lowers his voice further. "Four hours of

Elize might change your mind."

I laugh. "Mountains are possibly my most favourite thing in all creation. Even Elize can't ruin them for me."

"Your most favourite thing, huh? Better than the ocean?"

"Yes."

"Better than magical forests?"

"Yes."

"Better than ... zoo biscuits?"

I start laughing, but it fills me with a warm kind of glow that he remembers my zoo biscuit addiction. "Darn, I knew I forgot to bring something with on this hike." I step over a small pile of stones in the middle of our path, then ask, "What did Emily mean when she said you'd just been on a walking holiday?"

"Oh, yeah, I had a bit of a holiday before I came here. France first, then Switzerland, then Italy. In my last week I did one of those guided walking tours along the coast. That's what Emily was referring to."

"Wow, that sounds like an amazing holiday." An odd feeling that I quickly identify as jealousy pokes at my insides. "So you went with ..."

"Oh, it was just me. I, uh, felt like I needed a break from real life for a bit."

"You did all that on your own?"

"Yes. Well, aside from the many other tourists, but I gather that's not what you mean."

"And you didn't get lonely?"

"I thought I might, but it was surprisingly enjoyable

being left to make my own decisions. To only go where I wanted to go. Eat what I wanted to eat. It was great. I had a month off from reality and all the people I know, and by the time I got back home, I had a day left to pack for South Africa."

I stop walking and look at him. "And you did all that without once getting on a plane?"

He smiles. "Trains are a wonderful invention."

Up ahead, Matt decides we should stop for a few minutes to drink some water and admire the view. We catch up to the rest of the group, and Matt hands me my water bottle from the backpack he's been carrying. I take a few gulps, then place my hands on my hips as I turn back and look at how far we've come. The trees we walked through behind the lake are small, dark green blobs beside an uneven circle of blue that looks like a giant mirror.

"Beautiful," Aiden murmurs.

"Oh, it gets much better than this," I tell him. "The top is incredible. Like you've got the whole world at your feet."

Aiden looks somewhat alarmed. "Sounds high."

"Don't worry, man," Matt says. "It's totally safe." He packs my water bottle away and turns to look up the path ahead. "This next bit is steeper, but whoever built the path put logs across it, like stairs. So that helps."

"I'm leading now," Malcolm says, stepping past his brother and heading up the stairway of logs at a pace that seems far from enjoyable. "You've been in front for too long."

"Dude! You were right next to me!" Matt says, climbing

quickly after him.

"Hey, this isn't a race, remember," Emily shouts after them. "Or you'll be waiting at the top for hours before the rest of us get there."

She climbs after him, followed by Aunt Hannah, Elize, and Simone. Aiden gestures for me to go ahead of him. "So," he says after another minute or so of climbing, "was coming home as horrible as you thought it was going to be?"

"Well ... I still miss Julia a lot, but ... the other complication ... didn't turn out the way I thought it was going to." *And I still haven't figured out if I'm happy about that or not.* I glance behind me and see a perplexed expression on Aiden's face. Hardly surprising, since I probably couldn't have been more cryptic if I'd tried. I look forward again— just in time to trip over the next log. "Whoa—" I try to throw my hands out to break my fall, but Aiden grabs one of them first and pulls me upright. "Thanks," I say, wondering if the jolt of adrenaline rushing through me is from the shock of almost landing face first in the dirt or from Aiden's hand on mine.

"Everything okay down there?"

At the sound of Matt's distant shout, Aiden pulls his hand swiftly from mine. I look up, shielding my face from the sun's glare with one hand, and see Matt and Malcolm standing on the edge of a rock some way ahead of us. I give them a thumbs up and shout, "Yeah. Just me being clumsy." I wiggle my foot around to make sure it's still fine to walk on, then continue. "Anyway," I say to Aiden. "So coming home wasn't all that bad. The best part was probably finding a bag of biltong waiting for me on my bed." *Seriously? The best part was the* biltong? "And, you know, seeing my family," I add quickly. "Obviously."

"Biltong?" he asks.

"Yeah, you know. Dried meat. Salty. Spicy." When Aiden doesn't reply, I add, "Jerky, I think the Americans call it, although the South African version is obviously better."

"Oh, right," Aiden says. "I know what you're talking about."

"Do you like it?"

"I think it's one of the most revolting items of food ever created by man."

I turn around and stare at him with my hands on my hips. "What? It's delicious!"

"I'm sure it is," he says, wiping his face with the sleeve of his T-shirt. "To those who can stomach the idea of it."

"But it's *meat*. Real men like meat, don't they?" I say with a teasing smile.

He gives me that awesome grin of his. The one I haven't seen since the airport. The one that shows off his dimple. "Oh, I like meat. I just prefer it when it isn't both raw and shrivelled up at the same time."

I configure my face into an offended expression. "Biltong isn't shrivelled up."

"Whatever you say." He waves me forward with his hands. "Keep walking. We're getting left behind."

The large rock Matt and Malcolm were standing on marks the end of the log stairs. I fit my fingers into the cracks along the side and pull myself up, trying not to think about the excellent view Aiden currently has of my butt. I scramble onto the rock and stand. Aiden pulls himself up easily while I spot the next blue arrow painted on the rough surface next to my feet. It wouldn't have been a problem if I hadn't, though, because we could simply follow the sound of Simone whining about how hot it is and Elize telling her to stop being a baby.

"So, your sister's fiancé," I say to Aiden. "Do you like him?"

"Uh, yeah. He's cool. I'm happy for the two of them."

If I'm hoping to find out what that weird moment between Aiden and Emily was all about earlier, I'm probably going to have to be more direct with my questions. *You can do it, Sarah. Ask a personal question without messing up and having it come out totally weird.* "Um, earlier when we were in the lounge getting ready for the walk, Elize asked—"

"There you are," Matt says as Aiden and I climb around a boulder and find him and Malcolm sitting on a ledge sticking out over open space. Emily, Aunt Hannah, Simone, and Elize appear to be helping themselves to a box of biscuits from Matt's backpack. "You guys are taking forever."

"Stop exaggerating," Emily says. "We only got here, like, five seconds ago."

"Okay, fine," Malcolm says. "You're all taking forever, then. Matt and I have been sitting here for at least ten minutes."

"And we were watching those clouds over there and

thinking we should probably turn back," Matt adds.

I look to where he's pointing and see dark, heavy clouds gathering in the distance.

"What?" Elize says around a mouthful of biscuit. "Those clouds weren't there just now."

"That's what happens around here," Matt says as he climbs to his feet. "Storms appear out of nowhere in the afternoon, fling lightning, thunder, and buckets of rain all over the place, then disappear twenty minutes later. It's not something we want to get caught in."

"So that's it?" Aunt Hannah asks. "This is as far as we're going?"

"Yip. We could come back tomorrow, though, if you want to see the view from the top."

"*Nee dankie*," Simone mutters.

"Oh, no, that's all right," Aunt Hannah says. "I heard we might be having a relaxing day on the lake tomorrow." She zips up Matt's backpack and returns it to him.

"Down we go, then," Malcolm says, jumping up and pushing ahead of Matt so he can be at the front of the trail.

"Wait, Matt," I say. "Can I go just a little bit further? I want to see that foresty bit with the waterfall. Remember? It was so beautiful. Like a fairy land."

"Sarah, the storm's coming," Matt says with the tone of a long-suffering parent.

"I know, but it won't take long. Aiden can come with me, and we'll just be a few minutes behind you."

Matt crosses his arms. "Do you know the way?" he asks, looking concerned.

"Yes." I wish I could tell him not to speak to me like a child in front of all these people. "I remember this ledge from last time. Your mom waited here, and you and your dad and I walked a little further on and found that waterfall. Remember?"

Matt sighs. "Okay. I guess it's not that far from here. Anyone else want to go with Sarah and Aiden?" Matt looks around the group. No one says anything, although Elize gives him an are-you-kidding-me look. "Cool, well, we'll see you back at the bottom them," Matt says.

Aiden and I continue along the path, and after a few minutes, it slopes downhill and leads into an area thick with greenery. Leafy trees bend over our heads, their branches tangling together above us, and moss-covered stones line the muddy path. Water trickles not too far ahead.

"Isn't it beautiful?" I say to Aiden. "I can imagine fairies flying by and pixies prancing around. Tiny lights and sparkles of magic and circles of flowers and mushrooms."

Aiden chuckles. "It's certainly your kind of place."

I lead him between the trees until we get to a sheer face of rock with water streaming down it. The water dances and tumbles over stones before falling into a small pool that becomes a stream.

"Is this the waterfall you were talking about?" Aiden asks.

"Yes, but what I actually wanted to show you is off the path." I duck beneath a tree branch and climb over a damp log.

"Ah. I imagine your boyfriend wouldn't have been happy

to hear that."

I decide not to comment on that statement, mainly because it's true, but also because I don't want to get into a discussion about how it seemed like I had to ask Matt's permission just to walk somewhere. After fighting through a few more tangled branches and bushes, we come out onto a flat rocky surface. "Come and see," I say as I walk to the edge and look out across the spectacular landscape of rolling hills and mighty mountains. "We're a little sheltered here, so you can't see as widely as you can from the top, but the view is just as incredible."

"I think I'm going to stay here," Aiden says. I swivel around and see him hanging onto a tree branch as if it's the only thing connecting him to the earth, even though he's standing at least five metres from the edge of the rock.

"What's wrong?" I ask.

"Heights," he says. "I'm not a fan."

"Oh. I thought it was just flying."

"No. Not just flying."

"But ..." I turn back and marvel at the never-ending palette of green spread out before me. The bright green of the hills rolling into the darker green of the lower parts of the mountains spreading up into the grey-blue-green of the mountain peaks melting in the shadowy grey of the storm clouds. "You can't miss this view. It's magnificent. It's like opening a window from heaven and looking down at God's creation."

"That ... sounds amazing," Aiden says in a strained voice. "But you don't understand. The closer I get to the edge, the more it feels like the ground is tilting. Like it's getting steeper and steeper and I'm sliding towards the edge, and if I don't hold onto something I'll slide right off and plummet to the ground."

I pause for a moment, watching him, then say, "What if you hold onto me?"

He stares at me. I see the fear in his eyes. The same fear that was there when the plane took off. Am I only making things worse by trying to convince him to walk closer to the edge? But these mountains, this view … It's all so profoundly beautiful that it stirs something deep within me. Something I want to share with him.

I tilt my head to the side and say, "Come on. I dare you."

He raises an eyebrow at that. He lets out a long breath and says, "Okay. I guess I can't back down from a dare."

I walk back to him and hold out my hand. A thrill races through me as he takes it. A stupid, ridiculous thrill I have no right to feel. Step by step, we get closer to the edge of the rock. Aiden keeps his eyes aimed firmly upwards at the distant clouds as he mutters, "Don't look down, don't look down, don't look down." It makes me smile because it reminds of the things I like to chant to myself: *Don't be weird, just be normal. Say something, say something, say something.*

I stop, let go of his hand—with some difficulty due to how tightly he's holding onto it—and step in front of him. "Look over my shoulder. That way you can't look down. You can only look around."

We stand like that for some time. The clouds move closer, tumbling over each other in slow motion until they cover the sun. A cool breeze drifts over my arms, a welcome relief from the heat we were suffering under not half an hour ago.

"Okay," Aiden says eventually. "We should probably head back now."

I turn around, expecting him to have taken at least a few steps back by now, but he's right there, his face as close to mine as when he was about to kiss me in the airport. And that's all I can think about now, that kiss and his lips, which my eyes seem to be glued to. I wonder if he's thinking about the same thing. I wonder if he—

Crack!

The thunder gives me such a fright I almost fall backwards. Aiden grabs onto me and drags me back to the trees. "Yeah, we should definitely get going," I say.

We push through the branches until we get back to the muddy path. From there it's only a few minutes to the ledge where we said goodbye to Matt and everyone else. After that we hurry over rocks and logs, laughing at the fact that we were ever afraid of storms as children. Tiny spots of rain dot our skin and clothes, urging us on. I've never descended a mountain so quickly before, and I skid on loose pebbles and stumble over rocks far too many times. Aiden's always right there to steady me, though.

After a while, I start to wonder if we might actually beat the rain home. But then, with a fork of lightning that strikes alarmingly close by and a ground-shuddering crash of thunder, the clouds open and rain begins to bucket down. I come to a stop with a gasp, tensing against the cold water running down my back and drenching my clothes. But then, because it doesn't feel like there's any other way to respond, I start laughing. I turn around and find Aiden shaking his head at me. I can see he's trying to hold back a smile, though. "Oh, come on," I shout above the roar of the rain. "I've never been caught in the rain before. It's fun. And it won't be for too long. We should be quite close to the lake now."

I look around for a familiar landmark, but I don't spot anything. I turn slowly on the spot, feeling a twinge of apprehension in the pit of my stomach. "Um, do you remember this part of the hike from earlier?"

Aiden wipes a hand across his face and looks around. "Now that you mention it … I don't think so."

"And shouldn't we have come across another blue arrow by now?"

Aiden nods slowly, and when his eyes meet mine, I know he's thinking the same thing I am.

We're lost.

"BUT WE'RE STILL ON A PATH, AREN'T WE?" AIDEN SAYS,
looking at the ground. "So we can't be lost."

I shake my head. "There are rough paths all over the
place. That's why the hiking trails have different coloured
arrows painted here and there, so you know which one to
take. And they're a lot more clearly defined than this one. I
mean, the grass is barely flattened here, see? I doubt this is
part of any of the hiking trails." I look around once more as
anxiety grows within me. "I don't know where we are,
Aiden, and even if the storm passes quickly, it'll be getting
dark soon, and there are no lights out here, and neither of us
brought a phone or—"

"Hey." Aiden takes a step closer to me and touches my
arm. "Stop panicking. We're going to be fine. Think of this
as an adventure." He looks behind us, then ahead. "The way

I see it, as long as we keep going downhill, we're heading towards home."

"Yeah, I guess." I try to take Aiden's advice and stop panicking. "Unless we end up in the middle of someone else's fields."

"Then we'll just keep walking until we find a house, and we'll ask if we can use their phone." He grins. "I know how much you love talking to people you've never met before."

I groan and push him away from me. "Fine. Let's stay on this path, then. I suppose it has to lead somewhere."

Slippery grass and rocks hinder our progress, and raindrops pummel down with such force they sting my skin. So when we come across a stream with a number of trees growing along its edge, I take Aiden's arm and pull him beneath the tree with the largest, leafiest overhanging branches. "Let's just wait till the rain calms down a bit," I say. "I feel like it's attacking me right now."

"Good idea." Aiden sits on the ground, while I perch on the edge of a root. I try to ward off the chill by wrapping my arms around myself. This isn't Durban where the air is hot and heavy no matter what time of day or night it is. Up here in the mountains, when the sun disappears, the temperature drops.

"They're all going to be really worried about us," I say.

"Yes. Well, I'm sure *some* people will be worried about us."

I raise an eyebrow. "Meaning?"

"I have an aunt who isn't all that fond of me."

"But she wouldn't want you to go missing, would she? That's awful."

Aiden chuckles. "No, I'm exaggerating. We just tend to clash on a lot of issues, but she probably does love me deep down." He considers his words for a moment. "Very deep down."

"Is that the aunt who picked you up from the airport? The one who said she'd leave you behind if you weren't waiting for her when she got there?"

"Yes, that's the one."

"She's … your dad's sister?"

"Yeah." I hope he might say something about his dad this time, but he continues with, "That's who we're staying with—other than the time we're spending here. She lives in …" He pauses, clearly trying to remember the name. "Westville, I think it's called."

"Oh, okay. That's about twenty minutes from where I live."

Aiden smiles and shakes his head. "Weird, isn't it?"

"What?"

"We end up on the same plane—twice. We end up staying only twenty minutes away from each other. And then we end up at the very same family reunion. This holiday has been full of odd coincidences."

I shrug. "Maybe. If you believe in coincidences."

"You don't?"

I shake my head. "No. Not really. I don't believe that everything is just random. That everything happens by chance. I think things happen for a reason. Also," I add as I notice Aiden frowning at me, "Einstein agrees with me, and he was kind of a genius."

"Oh, well if *Einstein* agrees with you, then you must be right," he says with a laugh. He picks up a twig and starts scratching patterns into the dirt at his feet. "So ... you're saying it means something? These 'coincidences' involving you and me?"

I get the feeling I'm walking myself into an awkward situation here. "Um, I guess so."

He drops the twig and looks at me. "What does it mean?"

DEFINITELY AWKWARD. Because now he's staring deep into my eyes as if trying to find the meaning there, and I'm staring back trying to think of some kind of joking answer, but I can't, and my eyes won't look away, and all I want to say is that I don't know but it must mean SOMETHING, right?

Aiden is the first to break eye contact. He looks out between the dripping branches, and I realise as he does so that it's stopped raining. "That didn't last very long, did it?" he says. The storm has moved on, leaving us with nothing more than faint flickers of lightning and the distant murmur of thunder.

I clear my throat and stand up. "That's how it happens around here." I walk back to the path, wet dirt crunching beneath my shoes. The clouds are drifting away, revealing a purple-grey twilight sky. "We need to get moving. It's going to be dark soon."

Aiden jumps to his feet. "And that's when the monsters come out, right?"

"Hey, are you making fun of my overactive imagination?"

"Not at all. Cows can be very dangerous when caught in a bad mood. I'd better walk in front, just in case."

We follow the barely-there path as it leads away from the stream. My wet socks squelch uncomfortably inside my shoes, and my drenched clothing sticks to my skin. I rub my hands up and down my arms, but the goosebumps aren't going anywhere. It turns out getting caught in the rain isn't as fun as I thought it might be. At least, not when you wind up lost in the cold at the same time.

After about ten minutes, Aiden stops and says, "Hey, look what I spotted."

I look up, and between the trees ahead of us, I see— "The lake!"

"You see?" Aiden says. "We're not lost. We just took a detour."

Our detour seems to have brought us down the left side of the lake instead of the right. It's the side with the bench and the little wooden jetty. The side that *doesn't* lead to the hiking trail we started on earlier.

We step off the rough path and make for the trees, then walk around the edge of the lake. By the time we reach the other side and climb up the hill towards the farmhouse, it's almost dark. We cross the lawn we used for the party last night and climb the veranda steps. Through the glass sliding door, I can see the lounge is full of people, most of them standing, some talking on cell phones, all with anxious expressions on their faces.

"Oh! There they are!" Nan points at us, then hurries to the sliding door and opens it. "What happened?" she asks, pulling us both into a hug even though we're still soaking wet. She says something else, but her words are lost amidst the expressions of relief and Elize saying, "I'll go get towels," and Matt's mother saying, "Call Matt and the others and tell them to come back."

When Nan lets go of us, Aiden raises his voice and says, "Hey, sorry to worry you all. We ended up on the wrong path."

Someone groans, a few people laugh, and Matt's mother is suddenly beside me saying, "We were so worried about the two of you. All I could think of were those horrible stories of people getting lost in the mountains."

Elize returns with two towels. Nan takes them from her and hands us each one, then says, "Make sure you dry up properly. We don't want you getting sick. And now that you're both back, we should have dinner ready in about fifteen minutes."

"Oh! The stove!" Matt's mother dashes off in the direction of the kitchen, and Nan hurries after her.

I pull the towel around my shoulders while everyone who was gathered in the lounge gets back to whatever they were doing before they started panicking about us. I hear the front door open, and moments later Matt appears in the lounge doorway, his brother and father behind him. "Sarah," he says, his expression collapsing in relief. He crosses the room and wraps his arms around me, then lets go quickly once he realises just how wet I am.

"I'm sorry," I say. "I didn't mean …" My voice trails off as I look up and find anger in his eyes.

"What the hell happened, Sarah?" he demands. "You never should have gone off like that on your own, especially with a storm coming. That was a seriously stupid thing to do."

"Matt," I say quietly, glancing about awkwardly, "I'm fine. Everything's okay. And I wasn't alone."

"Oh, like getting lost with a foreigner in these mountains is any better than being on your own. What were you doing? Following the fairies in your head again? Why couldn't you just stick to the path?"

"Hey, it wasn't her fault," Aiden says, taking a step towards us.

"Oh, so does that make it your—"

"Oookay." Elize puts her arm around my shoulders and directs me towards the stairs. "You should probably have a shower so you aren't shivering the whole way through dinner. And you too, Aiden," she calls over her shoulder. "Although not *together*, obviously." Elize laughs at what she obviously thinks is a hilarious joke while flames of embarrassment engulf my face. I quicken my pace, dragging her up the stairs with me.

We reach our bedroom, and several seconds later Aiden walks past without looking at us. Elize leans in the doorway and watches him. She sighs. "I can't believe you got stranded in the rain with him. *Jy is so gelukkig.*"

I pause in my search for some dry clothes and look up at her. "You do remember you're related to him, right?"

"But if I were you, I wouldn't be," she says, turning her longing gaze on me. "How unfair is it that a totally hot and perfect guy shows up and it turns out he's my cousin?"

"Nobody's perfect," I say, though I think Aiden is pretty close. Or at least pretty close to being perfect for *me*. "I mean, he doesn't eat fish, which means he can never enjoy the gloriousness of sushi. And there's his over-the-top fear of heights and flying."

"Well, you can't exactly blame him for that, can you?" Elize says with wide eyes.

"I ... can't?"

"Of course not. Not after what happened to his dad."

I frown. "What happened to his dad?"

"You don't *know*?" Elize says, somehow managing to look horrified and gleeful at the same time.

"No, Elize, that's why I asked."

She closes the door and jumps onto her bed. "*O my genade*, it was *so* terrible. Well, it's not like I remember it happening, but the story sounds terrible. Aiden's dad was a pilot, and he was flying one of those small planes, and something went wrong when he was trying to land, and the plane just ... crashed. Like nose-dive crashed. The whole thing exploded and Aiden's dad and the three passengers were all killed."

I stare at her, my mouth open and my hand loosely covering it. "That's ... that is *horrible*."

"I know."

My hand drops to my side. "How old was Aiden?"

"Mmm … I think he was seven."

I shake my head as I think back to the way Aiden acted on the plane. No wonder he never wanted to get on one. I wouldn't either if that's how one of my parents died.

I gather my things and head to the bathroom. The hot water is deliciously warm against my cold, damp skin, but it doesn't distract me from the story I just heard. I'm still thinking about it when I leave the bathroom, and instead of going left towards the room I share with Elize and Simone, I turn the corner of the passage, walk to the end, and knock on the door.

"Yeah," Aiden calls out, which I take to mean 'come in.' I push the door open and find him sitting on the edge of a bed pulling socks on. His hair is wet, but he's wearing dry clothes. He must have used a different bathroom instead of waiting for me to finish. "Oh, hey," he says, looking surprised to see me standing in the doorway clutching a towel and a bag of toiletries.

"I … uh … Elize told me what happened to your dad, and … I just want to say I'm really sorry." I feel like I need to say something else, but I'm not sure what those words are supposed to be. So I end up standing awkwardly in the doorway wondering if I should wait for Aiden to respond or simply leave.

He gets to his feet and pushes a hand through his wet hair. "I probably should have told you. Then you wouldn't have had to wonder why I was being so weird on the plane."

I shake my head. "I didn't think you were being weird. I

liked the fact that you weren't all cool and confident."

He raises an eyebrow. "You don't think I'm cool?"

Damn that mouth of mine. I look down at the carpet as my face heats up. "I just mean that … it made it easier for me to talk to you."

When I peek up again, he's smiling at me. "I know," he says. "I'm just teasing you." He takes a deep breath. "Anyway, I'm glad Elize told you."

"You are?"

"Yes. It's not something I really like to talk about. I mean …" It's his turn to look at the carpet now, but not because he's embarrassed. It's as if he's looking through it, seeing something that isn't there. "I have memories. My mum tried to shield us from it all, but we saw things. Videos on the news. Photos in the newspaper. And talking about it brings up all those images in my head."

Crap, and now here I am talking about it!

"But I wanted you to know about it. So, yeah, I'm glad she told you."

I smile at him as a shout from downstairs informs us that dinner is ready. "I'll see you down there," I say, twisting around. I head back to my room with a lighter step. I don't know why, but it makes me happy that Aiden wanted me to know about his dad. It makes me feel kind of like … I matter to him.

I step into my bedroom—and surprise shoots through me at the sight of Matt sitting on one of the beds. He's leaning back against the pillows, his arms crossed over his chest. "I see you're getting to know my extended family quite well," he says. "Or one of them, at least."

I put my things down on top of my suitcase, then turn and face him. "You're talking about Aiden."

"Yes. The guy who managed to distract you so much that you got lost while coming down a perfectly visible mountain trail. The guy you were so desperate to talk to when you got out of the shower that you didn't even stop by your room first to put your things down."

I look down at my hands. "Elize told me what happened to his father. It sounded so … horrific. I couldn't stop thinking about it in the shower, so I went to talk to him afterwards. I just wanted to say that I was sorry about it. Because, you know, I didn't know before. And now I do."

Matt purses his lips, then says, "And the mountain? What happened out there?"

"Nothing *happened*. I showed him the forest and the waterfall and the view, and we were talking while we were coming down, and we somehow ended up on one of those smaller side paths that criss-cross all over the place. Then it started raining, and the rain was really heavy, so we sat under a tree till the storm passed."

"You sat under a tree during a storm?"

"Yes, we—Oh." I guess I really was distracted. "Look, it wasn't an isolated tree, and the lightning wasn't, like, right there."

Matt sighs as he climbs off the bed and comes towards me. "Sarah. You need to stop daydreaming so much and pay attention to what's going on around you." He rubs his hands up and down my arms. "And I'm sorry about earlier.

I was just so worried about you, and when I realised you were safe, I kind of overreacted." He leans forward and kisses my cheek, then takes my hand and leads me out of the room. As we head towards the stairs, I hear a creak in the floorboards beneath the passage carpet somewhere behind us, but when I look over my shoulder, I don't see anyone there.

From: Alivia Howard <livi-gem@gmail.com>
Sent: Sat 21 Dec, 11:25 am
To: Sarah Henley <s.henley@gmail.com>
Adam Anderson <ADA007@gmail.com>
Subject: The robots won't find us here

Squeeeeeeee! I'm gonna be home tomorrow night! I've missed you guys so much (and Logan too, but he's a gigantic butthead for ignoring all of us since we left school, so I've finally given up on trying to make contact with him). ANYWAY, you are hereby officially invited to my house on Tuesday. 10 am ish. Please respond with one of the following:

1) Yes
2) Yes!!
3) Oh, HELL YEAH, I'll be there.

As you can see, 'no' is not an option. I'll text you the code on Monday morning. See you on the other side!

xx Livi

P.S. Be ready for an overload of junk food. My hosts have insisted on feeding me rabbit food for the entire year.

From: Sarah Henley <s.henley@gmail.com>
Sent: Sun 22 Dec, 7:08 am
To: Alivia Howard <livi-gem@gmail.com>
Adam Anderson <ADA007@gmail.com>
Subject: Re: The robots won't find us here

My response: 1, 2 and 3! Can't wait to see you both!

P.S. I'll bring the zoo biscuits.

From: Adam Anderson <ADA007@gmail.com>
Sent: Sun 22 Dec, 7:43 am
To: Alivia Howard <livi-gem@gmail.com>
Sarah Henley <s.henley@gmail.com>
Subject: The robots will always find you

4) I'd rather have every hair on my body plucked out individually.
5) Kidding :) Obviously 1, 2 and 3.

P.S. I brought home a backpack stuffed full of American

choc / candy / biscuits / other life-threatening junk food. You're welcome, Livi.

P.P.S. I thought that most recent photo of you on Facebook looked suspiciously like a lettuce leaf ...

From: Facebook
<notification+oo425304@facebookmail.com>
Sent: Sun 22 Dec, 7:48 am
To: Sarah Henley <s.henley@gmail.com>
Subject: Aiden Harrison has accepted your friend request

I'm lying on my tummy on my slow-leak mattress typing a reply to Adam about how individual plucking of his hair can most certainly be arranged when the Facebook email about Aiden accepting my friend request pops up. Feeling a zing of anticipation shoot through me, I tap my way to my Facebook app and log in for the first time since I logged out on Friday morning. Now that we're officially Facebook friends, I can check out everything Aiden's posted on his wall. And that does *not* make me a stalker. Everyone does this. It's just one of the ways people get to know each other in the modern age.

Wait. Hang on. That probably means Aiden's checking out my profile. *Eeek!* I quickly go to my own page and scroll through it to see if there's anything overly embarrassing there. Aside from some less-than-attractive photos of Jules and me posing at various tourist destinations in London, my page seems fairly tame.

I navigate back to Aiden's page and start looking through his recent activity. He doesn't seem to be on Facebook too often, not like those people who post and comment and share and like *hundreds* of things every day. The most recent item on his wall is a digital artwork of a ship on a choppy sea with a woman standing at the bow looking out, her hair blowing back from her face. A dramatic sky is filled with orange, red, and dashes of purple, the colours reflected in the water. It's originally from a page called The Luminaire Artist, and Aiden's shared it along with one word: 'Awesome.' I have to admit, I agree. Sophie would definitely appreciate this.

I open a private message to her—no way am I sharing the image directly from Aiden's page, otherwise he'll know I came straight online to snoop around his profile—and type, 'Found this cool artist's page on FB. The Luminaire Artist. Kinda reminds me of some of your stuff. Check it out.'

I've just pushed 'Send' and gone back to Aiden's page when a shout from downstairs—"Breakfast is ready in ten minutes!"—reminds me that Nan said she was cooking a fry-up for everyone this morning. I drop my phone onto my pillow and jump off the mattress. I am so not sitting at the breakfast table with creased pyjamas and hair that looks like several mice crawled through it during the night.

I grab my shower stuff from my suitcase as Elize rolls over and mumbles, "Mmwawasthat?"

"Breakfast in ten minutes," I say, then run down the passage.

By the time I get back to the bedroom, she and Simone are gone. I hurry downstairs to the dining room and find the enormous table already crowded with people. Matt waves me over, and I slip into the seat he saved for me before everyone looks up to see who walked in late. The table is laden with plates of bacon, eggs, mushrooms, sausages, tomatoes, baked beans, and toast. Despite having already consumed a ton of food this weekend, my stomach grumbles in anticipation.

Matt squeezes my knee and says, "I'm glad to see your face doesn't look anything like Rudolph's."

I frown at him. "Rudolph?"

He gestures across the table. I look up, and when my eyes fall on Aiden, I start laughing. "Oh no! How did you get so burnt?"

Aiden touches his red cheeks and his even redder nose. "I thought I put sunscreen on, but I must have imagined that part."

"I guess your English skin just wasn't ready for our sun," Matt says. There's a tightness to his voice that matches his grip on my knee. He smiles at Aiden, but I know him well enough to know it isn't a genuine smile. "So," he says, turning back to me, "everyone seems keen to hang out by the lake today. Shall we take one of the rowboats out?"

"Uh, yeah, that sounds nice."

"Cool." Matt reaches for the nearest serving spoon and

starts dishing food onto my plate. "I guess you'll have to keep out of the sun today, Aiden" he says. "Wouldn't want that burn to get any worse."

Matt stays close to my side for the remainder of the weekend. He says it's because he wants to spend time with me after our weeks apart, but it kinda feels like he's watching me. By the time he and I leave mid Monday morning, I'm feeling rather smothered. Saying goodbye to everyone I know in the farmhouse takes a bit of time—and is hardly private—so I don't get to say much more to Aiden than 'Goodbye,' 'Nice to meet you,' and 'Maybe I'll see you again before you leave.' I half expect Matt to start interrogating me about my last words to Aiden the moment we're in the car, but he doesn't mention it.

"You know," I say once we're driving down the dirt road away from the farmhouse, "I could have driven myself here. Now you have to drive all the way back after dropping me off at home."

"It's fine," he says, his eyes on the road. "I like driving you around. Besides, I'm seeing an old school friend this evening. Wiggins. You remember him, right? So I'm only driving back here tomorrow."

"Christmas eve," I murmur, wondering how it snuck up so fast.

"Yip." Matt turns onto the tar road. "Big family

Christmas at the farm." He turns the radio up as a news broadcast comes on. I watch the mountains growing smaller and wonder if this is what the rest of my life will be like: Matt in the driver's seat and me doing little more to influence the direction of our journey than a passenger.

THE SUN BAKES THE ROOF OF MY TRUSTY OLD OPEL CORSA as it carries me along the coastal road towards Ballito on Tuesday morning. With no air conditioning, I'm forced to wind the window down to keep myself from melting. The air whips strands of hair across my face and fills the car with that distinctive smell of the sea. The ocean itself is startlingly beautiful. With barely a breath of wind to churn the crests of the waves into white horses, the water is a glistening stripe of deep blue, bleeding into almost-green as it reaches the shore.

I turn off the road and drive up to the imposing entrance of Zimbali Coastal Resort. As always, I feel completely awkward and out of place, as if I'm a lowly commoner trying to gain entrance to the royals' palace. My little car is like a piece of tin compared to Ostentatious Oversized Vehicle Number One that just drove past me and

Extravagant Expensive Vehicle Number Two that glides into the estate ahead of me beneath the residents' boom.

I pull up beside the guardhouse and wind my window all the way down as the guard walks over. "Hi, uh, I'm here to visit someone. I've got a code." I remove my phone from my handbag and find the message Livi sent me this morning. I show the screen to the guard, who leans down and squints at the numbers. He nods, then disappears back into the guard house where I see him speaking briefly on a phone. He returns and hands me a plastic access card.

"You know where to go?" he asks me.

"Yes. Thank you."

He opens the boom for me, and I drive beneath it. I follow the perfectly paved road past the resort and hotel area and towards one of the residential areas. All the houses are at least four times the size of my parents' house, but nestled amongst the trees and other expertly maintained vegetation, they somehow manage not to look so grandiose.

I make a few turns, drive beneath another boom—hence the access card I was given—slow down to allow a buck to leap across the road, and eventually arrive at Livi's house. I head up the driveway and park in front of the garage next to a white Jetta I recognise as Adam's mom's car.

Excitement races through me as I reach around to grab a beach bag from the back seat. It's only been a year since I saw my friends, but after having spent every day of high school with them, it's felt more like an eternity.

There were four of us—Alivia, Adam, Logan and I— who gravitated towards each other at the beginning of high school and formed one of the nerd herds. It would have been nice to be popular, of course, but as long as I had a few good friends I wasn't terrified of speaking to, I didn't mind what label I had.

At the end of high school, I decided to study in Pietermaritzburg with Matt, Logan went off to the gigantic, popular University of Cape Town, Livi got herself an au pair job with some noble family in Germany, and Adam went to America to spend the year working and travelling. Logan obviously became too cool to stay in contact with his nerdy high school friends, but Livi, Adam and I exchanged emails throughout the year. They told me all about their exciting experiences while I studied hard like a good girl and wished I had been brave enough to take an overseas gap year like they did.

I slam my car door shut and skip up to the front door. I consider knocking, but Livi always seems to be too far inside the house to hear me. I twist the knob and step inside the palatial home Livi's parents decided would be adequate for them and their only child. I leave my handbag and beach bag on the table in the entrance hall and head to the living area. It extends across the whole front of the house with nothing but floor-to-ceiling panes of glass separating the inside from the outside. Beyond the infinity pool in the garden, the golf course stretches out, blending into a line of blue sea at the horizon.

I hear laughter coming from the direction of the kitchen, and I follow the sound. I step through the doorway and find Livi sitting on a counter while Adam shows her something on his phone. She looks up as I walk in. "Sezziiieee!" she squeals.

"Liviiiiiii!"

"Eeeeeee!" Adam joins in the jumping up and down. "Let's all do the high-pitched, girly squeal thing!"

Livi punches his arm, and he falls all over the counter pretending to be injured while she runs across the kitchen and almost knocks me over with the force of her hug. "Sarah, Sarah, Sarah, don't *ever* let me leave the country again for so long."

I laugh and squeeze her tight. "Like I could ever stop you."

"I give you permission to tie me up," she says as Adam slings an arm around my shoulder and gives me a sideways hug.

"Ooh," I say, running my hand over his upper arm. "Did someone do some working out recently?" Adam is probably the ONLY guy in the whole world I can say that to without my face lighting up like a red traffic light. Five years of high school bonding will do that for you.

"I know, he is looking *so* good, right?" Livi says as she steps back to admire him.

"Sorry, ladies, but I'm already spoken for."

Livi laughs and puts her arm around me. "Don't worry, we wouldn't dream of stepping on Jenna's territory."

"Never," I add. Adam may turn out to be hotter than we could ever have predicted at school, but there's no way I can think of him as anything more than a friend or brother. "So, are we doing this pool thing?" I ask Livi. "I see you're all ready for the sun." Her naturally orange-red hair is scooped into a bun on top of her head, the tied ends of a bikini are sticking out at the back of her neck, and she smells like she used a whole bottle of sunscreen.

"Well, clearly I've got some catching up to do." She holds my tanned arm up and compares it to her pale one.

"You'll never be as brown as me," I tease. She sticks her tongue out, then crosses to the fridge and takes out three bottles of water.

"Where are your parents?" Adam asks.

"Oh, they're playing golf today, so we've got the house— and, more importantly, the pool—to ourselves."

"I'm just going to change," I call over my shoulder as I head out of the kitchen.

Several minutes later, I step outside and join Livi and Adam on the warm stone tiles beside the pool. I lay my towel out next to Livi's. Adam is on his stomach facing the two of us, and between our three towels sit a number of bowls of sweets, chocolates, and chips.

"Wow, you were serious about the junk food," I say, helping myself to a handful of M&M's.

"I'm always serious about chocolate," she says.

After a few minutes in which we all sample the contents from every bowl, Adam says, "So how was London, Sarah?"

"It was amazing," I say around a mouthful of cheese curls. "But I don't want to talk about London. I want to hear about Las Vegas and the Grand Canyon and your epic road trip and the summer camp you worked at. And Livi, I want to hear about the family you stayed with and the brats you looked after and whether they're actual, real-life royalty, and if you really did stay in an actual, real-life castle. And what about the BOY you mentioned?"

"Oh, total swoon!" Livi falls dramatically across her towel and dangles her hand in the pool. "You are going to love this story. Well, except for the ending. That part kinda sucked."

Adam groans. "Can't you keep the swooning-over-foreign-boys stories for a time when I'm *not* around?"

"Fine." Livi raises herself back onto her elbows. "The spotlight's on you then, Mr Anderson." She grabs her water bottle and holds in front of Adam's face like a microphone. "How is Miss Jenna Mackenzie?"

"Wait, I thought we weren't doing girly talk," Adam protests.

"Just answer the question, Mr Anderson," Livi says in her best Agent-Smith-from-The-Matrix voice.

Adam sighs, but a goofy grin comes over his face the way it always does when he talks about his girlfriend. "Jenna's awesome."

"She just finished matric, right?" I ask.

"Nope, matric this coming year. One more year until she can join me in the real world."

"You cradle-snatcher, you," Livi teases.

"Hey, we're only two years apart, okay."

"Which is, like, a decade in teenage years."

I throw a cheese curl at Livi, then turn back to Adam. "How did you guys handle having a whole year apart?"

"Well, you know, it was tough. Lots of Skype, mainly."

"Wasn't she crazy jealous about all the hot girls you were meeting over there?" Livi asks.

"Pff. What hot girls? You know nobody's hotter than Jenna."

"Ah, listen to him," Livi says with the tone of a granny admiring her adorable grandchild. "Isn't he just the cheesiest?" She picks up the cheese curl I threw at her and tosses it at Adam's head. It bounces off, lands on one of the stone tiles, and he promptly picks it up and puts it in his mouth.

"Ew!" I say through my laughter.

"Five-second rule," he tells me while crunching. "It's perfectly uncontaminated."

"And what about the twenty seconds it just spent next to Livi's towel?"

He shrugs. "You know I'm not a germophobe like you."

After some American stories from Adam and some German stories from Livi—and a dip in the pool to cool off before continuing our tanning efforts—Livi looks over to where Adam is lying on his back with a cap pulled over his eyes. "So, I've been thinking about next year, Adam, and I've decided that you and I can totally ditch our nerd image once we get to varsity. Clean slate. No more orchestra geek for me and no more skinny nerd for you." She pokes his almost-there six-pack, causing him to yelp. "Just don't make noises like that," she adds. "It isn't exactly macho."

"Hey, leave me out of this," Adam says. "I'm secure in my nerd status."

"Come on," Livi urges. "We can use Sarah as our example."

What? The water I'm drinking finds its way down the wrong tube, and I end up choking for a few moments. "Excuse me?" I say when I can breathe again. "How exactly am I the example of shedding one's nerd status and going on to become wildly popular?"

"Well, it wasn't *quite* like that," Livi says, "but you totally transitioned in matric after Mr Popularity asked you out."

I start laughing, which sets off the choking reaction at the back of my throat again. "I did not 'transition,' okay," I manage to gasp out between coughs. "It's not like I spoke to anyone else from the popular crowd. I never even sat with them or anything."

"Hey, you're ruining the story," Livi says. "Just accept that you went from nerd to cool, and we can do the same."

"But without having to date Mr Popularity," Adam pipes up from beneath his cap.

"Yes." Livi nods.

"Hey, that's my Mr Popularity you're making fun of." I squirt water at both of them, and Livi squeals while Adam does his non-macho yelp again. "Okay, truce, truce," I yell as Livi pulls off the cap of her own bottle and squirts water at my head. We both lay down our weapons and return to tanning on our towels. "Speaking of Mr Popularity," I say slowly, "why, uh, why do you think Matt still wants to be with me?"

Livi raises an eyebrow and Adam remains silent.

"Seriously. I'm not fishing for compliments here. I genuinely want to understand this. I mean, he's good-looking and smart and confident. He could have anyone he wants, so why me?"

"Seriously, Sezzie?" Livi says. "I mean, it's kind of obvious, isn't it?"

"It is?"

"Yes."

I stare at her, waiting for her to elaborate. "Well?"

"What, you want me to say it out loud?"

"Yes."

She stares at me a moment, then sighs and looks out across the pool. "Matt wants someone he can control. Someone who won't step out of line and embarrass him. And ... well ... you're easy to control. You're shy and quiet and you don't challenge him on anything. You're a whole lot of other things too, of course, like pretty and intelligent and kind, but mainly ..."

"I'm easy to control," I say quietly.

"I don't mean that in a bad way," Livi hurries on. "I just mean that you have the kind of personality that someone like Matt could take advantage of."

"Because I *let him* take advantage of me."

"Sarah ..."

Adam removes his cap and looks over at us, obviously sensing a shift in the mood.

"No, that's what you're trying to say, isn't it?"

"Okay, fine," Livi says. "Yes. You could stand up for

yourself sometimes. You don't have to do everything Matt tells you to do. You don't have to follow him around like a puppy craving love because you think so little of yourself that you don't believe anyone else could ever care for you like he does. You're worth more than that, Sarah. There are guys out there who are ten times better than he is. Guys who might actually deserve you. I wish you'd realise that and stand up for yourself and stop living in his shadow."

I stare at her, my mouth hanging open. Part of me realises she thinks she's being helpful, but I've never felt so hurt by her before.

"I don't have to listen to this," I mutter, standing up and grabbing my towel.

"Sarah, wait, come on. Just talk to—"

"Goodbye," I say without looking back.

"What? Are you leaving? You can't leave yet."

I step inside, grab my two bags, and hurry out to my car. Normally I'd change back into my clothes before leaving, but I don't want to be here another minute. I don't want to discuss what Livi said. I don't even want to think about it. I throw my things onto the passenger seat and slam my door shut before turning the engine on and revving far more than necessary in my attempt to get away quickly. I turn out of Livi's driveway, only glancing up at my rearview mirror at the last second. I see Livi standing at the open front door, Adam just behind her.

And then they're gone.

The whole way home, I expect to hear my phone ringing. I expect to answer it and hear Livi apologising for the things she said. But when I sit in the driveway at home and check my phone, there isn't even a message from her. There is one from Adam, though.

Adam: You shouldn't be asking yourself why Matt still wants to be with you. You should be asking yourself why you still want to be with him.

CHRISTMAS IS USUALLY A TREMENDOUSLY JOYFUL occasion, but I feel oddly subdued this year. Julia isn't here, Matt isn't here, I'm not speaking to my best friend, and Aiden hasn't made any kind of Facebook contact since he accepted my friend request.

After church, Sophie and I spend the remainder of the morning helping Mom in the kitchen. Aunt Maggie and Uncle Tom join us for lunch, along with some older relatives from Dad's side of the family. When we were younger, our grandparents always used to join us for Christmas, but they'd all passed away by the time I was fourteen. Our visitors spend all afternoon with us, and it's early evening by the time I get the chance to send Matt a text and thank him for the necklace he got me. He replies thanking me for the cologne.

Sophie and I lounge on the couch watching old

Christmas movies and picking at the leftovers from lunch until Mom and Dad shuffle down the passage to their bedroom, calling out "Goodnight" as they go. We look at each other, shrug, and turn the TV off. Sophie gets to her bedroom first, which means I'm left to lock up and turn the alarm on.

I drop into bed, already half asleep, and it's only then that I remember Aiden joking with me about arranging a secret rendezvous to exchange Christmas presents. I kinda wish we could have done that.

Matt: Hey babe. Sorry I didn't call to wish you merry Christmas yesterday. It's been kinda crazy at the farm with all the family here. Anyway, we're going to the aquarium at uShaka on Saturday. Want to come?

Sarah: Sounds cool. Who's going?

Matt: Does it matter?

Sarah: No, of course not. Just interested.

Matt: Sorry. I'm in a weird mood. Me, Malcolm, Emily, Aiden, Mom, Aunt Hannah and you, if you want to come.

Sarah: Cool. I'm in.

Saturday brings a killer sun. The kind of sun that makes your seatbelt so hot it'll give you first degree burns if your bare arm brushes against it as you slide into a car. The kind that gives you heat stroke and blistering skin if you dare to tan beneath it. The kind that leaves you wilting and begging for the cool breath of the storm that will almost certainly follow a day so horrifyingly hot.

I drape myself across one of the couches in the lounge and wonder why the one and only air conditioning unit we own chose *today* to give up. Then again, it was probably foolish to expect it to survive this kind of heat. It's at least ten years old, after all.

I lift my head high enough to see the clock on the wall— half an hour until Matt picks me up—then drop it down again. Seriously, I had no idea my head was this heavy. How on earth do I manage to carry it around every day?

Ding dong!

The sound of the doorbell startles me, mainly because it doesn't get used that often. Everyone who lives here has keys to get in, and everyone who visits has to stand at the gate at the bottom of the driveway and push the buzzer, so by the time they get onto the property, we've already opened the front door.

I wait a few seconds, hoping someone else from my family might check who it is, but I hear no hint of movement in the house. I climb onto my feet, and everything goes white for a moment before coming back into focus. "Stupid heat," I mutter. My strength is completely sapped. I'm weak simply from standing up and walking to the front door. I hang onto the door handle and blink a few times before pulling it open.

My vision goes white again, and this time I almost pass out.

"Hi," Aiden says, raising his hand in a semi-wave. "Good to see you haven't melted yet."

I blink again. It's definitely Aiden. The sunburn that covered his face a few days ago has faded, leaving his skin a golden brown. I guess he's one of those lucky people whose skin doesn't peel after it burns. *Focus, Sarah. WHAT IS HE DOING HERE?* "I—um—how—what are you doing here?"

"Did you know your gate is open?" Aiden gestures over his shoulder.

I let out a very unladylike "Huh?", but since I'm seriously considering the fact that I did actually pass out and am now dreaming, it doesn't bother me too much.

"Yeah, I thought I'd just mention it, since you South Africans are kinda pedantic about your gates and security and stuff."

"Uh huh." This is definitely weird enough to be a dream.

"And why didn't you tell me you live opposite a cemetery? That's seriously cool. Must have made for some awesome ghost stories when you were little."

"Uh …"

"Oh, sorry, you asked what I'm doing here. My aunt was

147

supposed to drop us off at Matt's, but we got there a bit early, and no one was home. I called Matt and it seems he's still at gym, so I asked him for your address."

"You … what?"

"Yeah, I know. He was *ecstatic* about that." Aiden rolls his eyes. "I guess he isn't wild about me spending time with you since I led you astray on a mountainside and got you stranded in a storm."

I wipe a hand across my sweaty forehead. "So … I'm not dreaming?"

Aiden laughs. "I don't think so. Not unless I'm dreaming too."

"And …" I try to remember what he said. "Did you say 'us'?"

"Uh, yes. Emily and my mum got excited about a flower in your driveway. Something to do with wedding bouquets."

"Right." I lean past him and see Emily and Aunt Hannah on the other side of the driveway bent over a bush. "Uh, well, come in."

I push the gate button on the wall beside the front door—because, as Aiden pointed out, we're pedantic about security around here—and step back to let him in. *Crap, what does the house look like? What does my* room *look like? No, why would he be going into my bedroom? He wouldn't. Don't be ridiculous.*

"Sorry to just show up like this," Aiden says. "I can tell it's got you all flustered."

"What? No. I'm not—"

"Don't even try," he says with a grin. "I haven't known you for that long, but it's been long enough to know that you're completely flustered right now. You shouldn't be, by the way. It's just me."

I pause for a moment to remind myself that he's right. I already did this whole freaking out thing on the plane; it doesn't need to happen again. I look up at him with what I hope is a coy smile. "Maybe it's not you. Maybe it's actually the heat."

"Of course. How vain of me to think I might have been the reason." He tries to keep a straight face. "Does this kind of heat always fluster you?"

"Uh, no," I admit as I wander into the lounge with Aiden just behind me. "It usually leaves me draped over an item of furniture in a useless, sticky mess. Which is the state I was in before you rang the doorbell." I wipe my sweaty hands on my shorts. "And it's what I still sort of … seem to be."

"I think everyone's a sticky mess right now," Aiden says. "I've certainly never experienced anything like this."

"Would you like some iced water?" I ask, heading for the kitchen. "It's the only thing I drink when it gets this hot."

"Yes, that would be great, thank you," he says. It doesn't sound like he's following me, though. I turn back and see him looking at the collection of family photos on the wall. Well, I suppose it can't hurt to leave him there for a few minutes. The photos aren't *too* humiliating.

I move slowly around the kitchen, filling two glasses with water and breaking a few ice blocks from the tray I refilled last night. Then I think about Emily and Aunt Hannah outside and figure they might want some water too, so I take out another two glasses. When I eventually walk back into the lounge carrying all the glasses on a tray, Aiden is nowhere to be seen. I set the tray down on the coffee table and look out the door to the garden. Sophie is lying on a yoga mat beneath a tree with a pencil in her hand and a sketchpad in front of her, but there's no Aiden. I walk back to the front door and peer out. Emily and Aunt Hannah are having an animated discussion about something, but Aiden isn't here either.

"Weird," I mutter to myself. Perhaps he went in search of a bathroom. I walk down the passage to see if the bathroom door is closed, but before I can get there, I pass my bedroom. And there's a tall male figure standing at my desk. With one of my notebooks in his hand. Open. He turns the page just as I blurt out, "WHAT ARE YOU DOING?"

He jumps, drops the notebook, and swings around with a hand on his chest. "I ... uh ... your bottom drawer was open."

"And you thought that was an invitation to help yourself to its contents?" My hands are shaking. Mainly from an overload of embarrassment, but I suspect there's some anger in there too. A small amount of outrage at having my privacy violated, even though it's Aiden, and he's probably one of the few people I'd actually allow to read my notebooks if I were forced to pick someone.

"Well, uh ..." Guilt is written all over his face, so it's clear he knows he shouldn't have been touching my stuff. "I saw the notebooks. And I figured they were full of your stories. And I was curious ..."

I take a step back and point down the passage. "You need to get out of my room."

"Right. Yeah. Of course." He slides past me and hurries back towards the lounge. I wait in the passage for a bit, trying to contain my mortification. I wish I knew which pages he read. How bad were they? Ugh, I'm DYING! This is SO EMBARRASSING! No one is supposed to read the rubbish I scribble down!

I slowly enter the lounge and sit down without meeting Aiden's gaze. He's doing that nervous tap with his fingers on the armrest of the couch, just like he did on the plane. "I'm so sorry," he says. "I shouldn't have gone into your room, much less touched your notebook."

"Let's never talk about it." I'm still staring at the floor. I hope I never have to know what he was thinking while reading those pages.

"But, Sarah," he says, "it was really good. Whatever story I was reading, it was very—"

"Stop," I say, finally looking up. "Everything in that notebook is a rough first draft, okay? It's so far from perfect that I'm the only one who should ever read anything in there. So don't try to make me feel better about this gigantic embarrassment by telling me that what you read was actually *good*."

"But ..." Confusion crosses Aiden's face. "I'm giving you my honest opinion. I only read a few pages, and no, they weren't *perfect*, but the story was gripping and the characters were intriguing. I wouldn't have kept turning the pages if I wasn't—"

"Okay." I stand up and grab one of the glasses from the tray. I take a long gulp before returning it to the table. "We, uh, need a change of subject. I … I was going to show you something. Yes, that's what I was going to do." I run to the kitchen, using up the small burst of energy provided by the iced water, and rummage in a cupboard for the rectangular package with colourful images of cartoon animals painted onto its blue surface. I return to the lounge. "These," I say, holding the package up, "are zoo biscuits."

Aiden lowers his glass and looks up. "Oh. Cool." He seems more relaxed now that I'm no longer ordering him out of my room or telling him how dreadful my stories are. "Do I get to taste them?" he asks.

"Yes." I sit on the couch beside him and tear open the packaging. I slide the plastic tray containing the biscuits out and tip it upside down on the coffee table, spilling the biscuits across its surface. Part of me panics about the crumbs going everywhere, but I tell my neat-freak side to take a break.

"Wow, they're quite bright," Aiden says, picking up a biscuit covered in blue icing with a white dolphin shape on top.

"Yeah, so if you have any kind of food colouring allergy, speak now."

Aiden examines the biscuit. "Well, if I didn't before, I might after eating this."

"Hey." I nudge his knee with mine. "They aren't *that* bad."

"Uh huh."

"Well, are you going to taste it or not?"

"Wait, I haven't checked all the animals yet. I need to be sure I've picked my favourite." I roll my eyes as he examines the various colours and shapes. "Okay, so we've got dolphin, a flying duck, a bear, a ..."

"Springbok," I say.

"Right. And ... some other shape I have no hope of identifying."

"It's a squirrel," I say with a laugh.

"There is no way that's a squirrel."

"It is. Look." I pick up the green covered biscuit and turn it so the squirrel is sitting upright.

"Hmm. You may actually be right." As he tries to take the biscuit from me, his fingers brush against mine, and I don't seem to be able to let go. My eyes find his, and once our gazes are locked, I have no hope of looking anywhere else.

So there I am, my fingers glued to the stupid biscuit and my eyes glued to Aiden's face. And I'm pretty sure I'm imagining it, but I think his face might be coming closer to mine. *No, no, no, this isn't good. Not good. Not good. Don't do it.*

"Hello-o?"

As if someone flipped a switch, my hand drops from the biscuit and I jerk away from Aiden. He looks startled, as if he just woke up from a daydream.

"Anyone here?" The shout is coming from the entrance hall. I jump up—whoa, too fast, too hot, head spinning, DON'T pass out!—sway for a moment, then navigate my way out of the lounge without falling over. Emily and Aunt

Hannah are standing at the open front door peering inside. I'm about to walk over to them and welcome them inside when my mother rushes down the passage patting her hair. Before I know it, she's at the door greeting the two of them, finding out who they are, introducing herself, and apologising for hiding out in her bathroom because it's the coolest room in the house right now. She's just inviting them into the house when a honk outside makes them all look out the door.

"Matt and Malcolm are here," Mom calls over her shoulder.

I turn and look back at Aiden. He's munching on something while returning the zoo biscuits to the plastic tray. When he walks over and joins me in the doorway, I say, "Well, what do you think?"

"It was … very sweet."

I roll my eyes and head to my room to fetch my bag.

Malcolm drives Matt and me, and his mother takes Aiden, Emily, and Aunt Hannah. When we climb out in the parking lot at uShaka Marine World, Aiden, Emily and their mother are arguing.

"... won't talk to me about it," Aunt Hannah is saying.

Aiden lets out a frustrated breath of air and says, "Can I have my phone back now?"

"I just think you should call her," Aunt Hannah says.

"No, Mum, he does *not* need to call her." Emily snatches the phone from her mother's hand and drops it into Aiden's back pocket.

"I just think that if there's a chance—"

"No, Mum," Emily says. "I know you don't believe me, but I've told you before how she—"

"Look, it's actually no one else's business except mine," Aiden says. "So I'd appreciate you both keeping your prying eyes away from my phone." He strides away from us towards the entrance.

I shoot a questioning look at Malcolm, but his only answer is a shrug. I look at Matt, but he only just climbed out of the car after putting the sun reflector over the dashboard and doesn't seem to have heard the argument.

We cross the parking lot and climb the stairs to where Aiden is standing in front of the enormous open jawbone that welcomes visitors to uShaka Marine World. It's a replica of an ancient species of shark. A megalodon, I think it's called. Emily and Aunt Hannah exclaim over the sheer size of the thing, and Emily gets her camera out. I walk to Aiden's side and quietly ask, "Is everything okay? I didn't mean to eavesdrop, but I kinda heard ... back in the parking lot ..."

He smiles at me. "It's nothing. Just a ... complication from back home. It doesn't matter."

I nod, wondering what the complication's name is and how close she and Aiden are.

After taking a few group photos in front of the megalodon jaw, we head for the aquarium entrance. Matt takes my hand and holds onto it firmly, as though I might run away if he lets go. Once we've passed all the shops and restaurants and arrive at the Sea World entrance, Matt and his mother examine the board with the ticket prices. They have a brief discussion, then Matt turns to the rest of us. "Okay, so we were going to get tickets for both Sea World and Wet 'n Wild, but since it's dangerously hot today, I think we should just do Sea World."

"Which is ... the aquarium?" Emily asks.

"Yes. Largest aquarium in the Southern Hemisphere," Matt says proudly, as if he had something to do with it.

"Wet 'n Wild?" Aiden whispers to me, his eyebrows raised. "Isn't that a brand of—"

I elbow him in the ribs before he can say it. I clear my throat and say, "It's the water slides and tubing and stuff like that."

He smirks at me. "They could have given it a less dodgy name."

"Or you could just get your mind out of the gutter," I suggest.

Matt frowns at me, and I wonder how much he overheard. I step away from Aiden and pull my hand out of Matt's grip so I can get my purse out to pay for a ticket. I should probably keep away from Aiden as much as I can today so Matt doesn't end up exploding.

"It's *inside* a ship?" Emily squeals as we walk down the ramp into the aquarium. "That's amazing."

"Yes, they constructed the whole thing as if it's an upside-down shipwreck," Matt's mother tells her. "The aquarium tanks are all built in as part of it, so you walk through the ship to view them." She continues telling Emily and Aunt Hannah everything she knows about the aquarium, while I focus my full attention on the cool air blowing across my skin. *Thank you, God, for properly functioning air conditioners.*

We begin winding our way through the ship's interior, allowing ourselves to be dazzled by every shape, size, colour and pattern of fish. I have mixed feelings about aquariums. I don't like the shows they put on with dolphins and penguins and things, because I've heard horrible stories of how those animals are treated sometimes. But the display tanks built into the shipwreck are incredibly beautiful, and I hope I'm not deluding myself by imagining they feel just like the real ocean to the sea creatures who inhabit them.

I stop beside one of the tanks and run my hand along the wall. A wall that mimics the rusted metal interior of a shipwreck. I imagine a storm at night, the ship tossed about in violent waves and the crew falling all over the place. Unceasing forks of lightning tear through the sky, and thunder loud enough to rattle the bones of the dead reverberates through the ship's skeleton. Jagged rocks hide beneath the water's choppy surface, getting closer and closer. The ship rams into them, flinging its helpless crew across the deck. The hull fills with water. The crew try desperately to save their ship, but it's too late. The water is flooding in faster, and people are screaming, and the ship is—

"Sarah, come on." I blink and find Matt coming back around a corner with Aiden just behind him. "You're getting left behind," he says with a sigh, taking my hand and pulling me after him. We join the rest of our group, and Matt jumps into the discussion about the Nemo/Dory tank as if he's been part of it from the start. Nemo and Dory. Now there's a good story. I wonder if Aiden's seen the movie. My gaze moves to him, and I'm startled to find him watching me. I raise my eyebrows in question.

He laughs quietly to himself. "I understand now."

"Understand what?"

"How you almost missed a flight. You were doing it now, weren't you? Watching a story play out in your head. I saw how you totally zoned out."

"I …" I shake my head. "I really need to stop doing that."

"Yes, you do," Matt says, giving me a small smile. I hadn't realised he was listening to us. "Otherwise you might end up zoning out while driving a car one day, and who knows what could happen then." He kisses my cheek, then adds, "You didn't tell me you almost missed a flight, babe. When was that?"

"Um, oh, it was … from Dubai to Durban. But it was fine. I made it in time."

I keep a hold on my imagination for the remainder of our journey through the aquarium, and Matt keeps a hold on my hand. When we're out in the sun again, Matt turns to his mother and says, "Should we have lunch somewhere while we're here?"

"I was about to suggest the same thing," she says. "And I don't mind where we go as long as it has air conditioning."

"That Moyo place looked cool," Emily suggests.

Matt makes a face. "It's not as good as it used to be. Oh, there's a Cape Town Fish Market next to it, though. How about that?"

I frown and bite my lip. I want to point out that the Cape Town Fish Market is a rather pricy restaurant, especially since we just forked over a large amount of money for the ticket into the aquarium. But we didn't end up going into the Wet 'n Wild section, so I guess I can afford to splash out on my meal. I nod along with everyone else, but then I remember another reason we shouldn't eat there. "Oh, Aiden doesn't eat fish."

Matt looks at his cousin. "Is that true?" he asks in a tone of voice that might suggest he's interrogating someone about a crime they committed.

"Uh, yes," Aiden says. "But I'm happy to go there if everyone else wants to. I'm sure they have other stuff on their menu."

We settle into a booth, and I find myself squished awkwardly between Aiden and Matt. WHAT THE HECK? I thought I'd carefully arranged the timing of my sliding onto the seat so I'd end up next to Emily. How did Aiden get past his sister? Now I've got his leg pressed against me on one side, and Matt's leg pressed against me on my other side, and I'm a sweaty mess in the middle—because no amount of air conditioning can help me now.

I try to distract myself with the menu, but my legs feel like they're burning up. Seriously, when did these booths get so small?

"What you gonna have, babe?" Matt asks me.

"Uh, I'm not sure yet." How about a bowl of ice cream to cool down my burning body? No, wait, I don't think my stomach can handle something so sweet right now.

"Have some sushi," Matt says.

"Um …" I eye the prices next to the sushi and think

about how I spent almost all my savings getting myself across the world to visit Julia.

"Just get some. I know you love sushi."

"Okay." I see my chance to escape for a few minutes. "I'll go see what plates they've got on the conveyor belt thingy." Matt moves so I can get past him, and I just about crawl across the seat in my desperation to get out.

"I'll come with you," Aiden says, giving Matt a suspiciously wide grin as he shuffles across the seat. I start to wonder if Aiden's doing all this—arriving early and getting dropped off at my house, whispering to me, sitting next to me, accompanying me to the oh-so-far-away sushi bar—just to annoy Matt. Maybe this has nothing to do with me. Maybe he's been pissed off at Matt ever since the mountain incident, just like Matt's been pissed of at him, and the two of them are trying to see who'll break first.

I stalk away from the table without waiting for Aiden. He joins me at the sushi bar a few moments later. He opens his mouth to say something, then hesitates. With a frown, he asks, "Is something wrong?"

I take a deep breath and shake my head. I'm too scared to confront him. I'm too scared to confront anyone about anything.

"Okay," Aiden says, though I can tell he doesn't believe me. "Well, I'm here for my sushi lesson. Tell me everything you know, Master Sushi-Eater. Not that I'm going to join you in eating it, of course. I just thought it might be time to educate myself in The Ways of the Raw Fish."

Despite my frustration, I can't help smiling at the rubbish spurting from his mouth. So I point out the various types of sushi on the plates travelling around the bar and explain what's in each of them. By the time I'm finished, I still haven't decided which one I want. I look around and notice some unusual sushi on a table nearby. "I wonder what those are."

Aiden turns and leans against the bar. "Go and ask."

"What?"

"Go over there, politely interrupt that young couple, and ask what kind of sushi that is."

I stare at him in horror. "There's no way I'm doing that."

"Come on." He leans closer to me with a glint of mischief in his eyes. "*I dare you.*"

That moment on the mountain comes rushing back to me. I'm standing at the edge, holding my hand out to Aiden, saying the exact same words to him. And he did it. He walked to the edge.

But this is different. There was no one on the mountain for Aiden to be embarrassed in front of, but there's a restaurant full of people here. I'm going to stand in front of that couple and make a total fool of myself when I go blank and no words come out of my mouth.

"No," I say, turning back to the coloured plates of sushi travelling on the conveyor belt.

"Sarah, if you don't try, you're never going to get any—"

"No!" I grab the nearest two plates and escape back to the booth. I have to wait for Aiden to return before Matt and I can slide back onto the seat, but I don't make eye contact with him when he does. We don't say anything to each other for the remainder of lunch, and, somehow, his leg stays far away from mine.

After lunch, the other three ladies disappear to find a bathroom, while Matt tells the rest of us he wants to check out the shark cage diving. Apparently he's planning to do it the next time his friend Wiggins visits. I ask for Malcolm's keys and tell Matt I don't feel too well and will wait in the car for everyone.

I wrap my arms around my chest as I head past the shops and cafes towards the parking lot. The weather is changing, and a cool breeze brushes over my skin. My brain tells me I shouldn't be feeling cold—I mean, this is *Durban* for goodness sake; a cool breeze in summer does not equal cold—but I'm shivery nonetheless.

"Hey, Sarah, wait for me."

I stop by the megalodon jaw and look back. I frown when I see Aiden jogging towards me. I was hoping for a few quiet minutes alone in the car. "I thought you were checking out the shark cage diving."

He stops in front of me and lifts one shoulder in a half-shrug. "I wanted to see if you're okay."

"I'm fine," I say automatically.

"Are you still upset because I dared you to speak to those people?" he asks. "Look, you pushed me to face my fear when we were up on that mountain, so I figured I'd push you to face yours. But I guess it wasn't the right time for you."

I shake my head and pretend to examine the oversized teeth inside the ancient sea monster's jaw. "It's not just that."

"Then what?"

I let out a frustrated breath. "Are you *trying* to get me in trouble with Matt?"

"I don't know. Are you *trying* to let your boyfriend control every aspect of your life?"

I look at him, my mouth dropping open the same way it did after Livi's little speech. And just like then, my first instinct is to run. I don't want to have this argument. I don't want to fight with Aiden. I don't want to fight with *anyone*. I bite my lip, then say, "We don't need to talk about this."

"Actually, I think we do. Or *you* do, at least. If not with me, then with someone else."

I start walking. "I'm going to the car."

"Do you run away from *every* form of confrontation?" he demands, his words stopping me in my tracks. "Because *God*, that is annoying."

I turn back to him. My hands are shaking, but I manage to keep myself composed. "Thanks, but my name's not God."

"I—it—that's just something people say, okay?"

"I know. There are a whole lot of people talking to God and they don't even know it. Don't you think that's weird?"

His tanned face turns slightly red. "That's not the point!"

"I know. Your point is that you think I do everything my boyfriend tells me to do, and I'm trying to distract you from that because I don't want to argue about it. You have to admit, though," I continue before he can get another word in, "that it's weird how so many people talk to a God they don't even believe exists. But you know what would be even weirder? If he *spoke back*. Like real, audible words. Just imagine it: A guy is walking down the street and he stops to light a cigarette. He accidentally burns himself and yells, 'God, that hurt!' And the clouds part above him and a great, booming voice says, 'I know, son. You know what else hurts? Dying from lung cancer. This is a sign for you. Stop smoking.'"

Aiden stares at me as though tentacles are sprouting from my forehead. He shakes his head. "You can come up with as many stories as you like, but that doesn't change the fact that you don't have a clue what you want in life and you're happy to sit back and let other people tell you what you should want."

"Excuse me?" I shout, anger slipping past my calm facade.

"You couldn't even figure out what you wanted for lunch! Your boyfriend had to tell you what to eat."

"Oh, for crap's sake, that was just *lunch*, Aiden. It means nothing."

"It's not just lunch. It's everything. You had to ask your boyfriend's *permission* just to walk a little further up the mountain. He drove you to and from the Drakensberg because he didn't think you could handle the drive on your own."

"Hey, that was not the only reason he—"

"You didn't want to go to that restaurant today, but Matt wanted to, so that's where we went. I bet the only reason you're studying in Pietermaritzburg is because Matt suggested you go there with him. And you don't want a career in science, Sarah, so *why are you studying science*? Is it because that's what both your parents do?"

"Stop it!" I yell at him. "Maybe it's okay not to know what I want yet. Not everyone has their whole life figured out at age nineteen."

"No, they don't. But most people have the sense to let go of the things they *don't* want."

"What exactly are you trying to say?"

"You don't want to be with Matt," he shouts, "so why are you hanging onto him?"

"I … maybe I do." My voice comes out all wobbly, and I hope I don't start crying now. "He … he takes care of me. He makes me feel safe. How is that possibly wrong?"

"Because it's not the right kind of safe, Sarah. A bird is safe when it's closed in a cage, but it isn't *living*. It isn't *flying*. You have beautiful wings desperate to stretch out and catch the wind." He steps closer to me. "Don't. Let. Anyone. Stop you."

"And what happens," I whisper, "when I fall?"

"Then you have someone waiting to catch you," he says gently. "That's the right kind of safe."

I bite my lip, trying desperately to figure out who it is that's supposed to catch me if it isn't Matt.

"Be brave," Aiden says. "Take a chance. Spread your wings."

I shake my head and back away from him. "That isn't me. I've never been brave." I turn and run down the steps towards the car.

My throat is scratchy and sore, and my nose won't stop dripping. At first I thought it was due to all the crying I did this evening, but the two jerseys I'm wearing and the five gazillion sneezes that have attacked me in the past hour have led me to a different conclusion: I'm getting sick.

I climb beneath my duvet and close the window next to my bed so the sound of bucketing rain isn't so loud. I find my phone amidst the folds of blanket and search for the number of the one person I want to speak to right now. I snuggle against my pillows and listen to the ringing. *Please answer*, I think. *Please answer, please answer, please—*

"Hello? Sarah?" Livi says breathlessly, as though she had to run to get to her phone.

"Hey," I say, picturing her having a fantastically fun evening without me. That would explain why her phone was far away and she had to run to it. Maybe I should end the call right now before we have a conversation that makes me feel even worse.

"Um, hi," she says. "I was starting to think you weren't going to return my call."

My forehead creases. "Uh ... what call?"

"Oh." There's a pause. "Didn't Sophie give you the message?"

"No. She's been out all evening. I haven't seen her."

"Oh. Well, I called you on the landline earlier. Because, um, I thought it might end up being a long conversation, and, you know, free landline calls on weekends and all that."

"Oh yeah. You're right." With the gaping hole in my bank account, I should have thought of that. "That's a good idea. I'll call you back." I end the call and climb out of bed. I shuffle down the passage in my slippers and fetch the cordless landline phone.

A minute later, I'm back in bed dialling Livi's home number, which I've known by heart since we were in Grade Eight. She answers after one ring. "Hey."

"Hey." I rush straight into the apology before I can chicken out. "I'm really sorry about the other day. I shouldn't have overreacted and run off like that."

"No, I'm sorry. I shouldn't have said those things."

"You were right, though."

"Well, yeah, I was," she says. "But I shouldn't have said it like that. I could have been a lot more—Wait, did you say I was right? Ohmygosh, did you break up with Matt? SARAH! You can't go for so long without talking to me! I've been dying here trying to figure out if I should call you or not. What happened? What did I miss?"

I start laughing, then grab a tissue from my bedside table to mop up my continuous nose-dripping. "No, I didn't break up with Matt. But today someone told me pretty much the same thing you told me—well, he actually shouted it at me—and I figured that if it's obvious to someone I've known forever, and it's obvious to someone I just met, then maybe it should be obvious to me too. So I started thinking about it, like *really* thinking about it, and ... I guess Matt *is* super controlling. And ... maybe a little possessive and ..." Probably a few other things too, but Livi doesn't need to know what happened the night before I left for London. "Anyway, it's probably all stuff we could work through together if I actually wanted to be with him, but I'm not sure I do."

"Really? So what are you going to do? And wait, who is this 'he' you just met who was shouting at you about Matt?"

I let out a long sigh. "I think I need to tell you what happened on my flight back from London."

"Ooh, yes, please do. Is this a good story?"

"Yes," I say with a smile.

"Great. I've got popcorn."

I start laughing again. "Seriously?"

"Yes. I was watching a movie before you called, so I'm all ready with the snacks."

I slide down a little further in my bed and start telling Livi all about Aiden. Popcorn crunches in my ear, punctuated by the occasional 'What?', 'Seriously?' and 'Ooh!'."

"Okay, so this Aiden guy sounds pretty amazing," Livi says when I'm done telling my story.

"Yeah, but ... I don't know. I think he might have some relationship complications of his own—" I still need to find out more about the 'she' Emily and Aunt Hannah were referring to "—and he's returning to England next Friday, so then what? Even if he wants to be more than friends, it would all be long distance, and that sucks. And why am I even saying any of this, because I'm technically still dating Matt!"

"So ... here's how I see it," Livi says. "The decision isn't 'Matt or Aiden.' The decision is 'Matt or no Matt.'"

"Yes. Wow. That makes a lot of sense, actually. How did you become so wise, Liv?"

"I have my moments."

"It seems obvious what I should do, but then ..." I groan. "Then I start thinking about Matt's family and how awesome they are, especially his grandparents, and if I break up with him, I'll never see them again, and—"

"Like I said," Livi interrupts. "Matt or no Matt. That's it. Leave his family out of it. As nice as they may be, they're not the ones you're dating. And it might be sad if you can't see them anymore, but you can't stay in a relationship with Matt just because you want to see his grandparents."

With a sigh, I say, "I know. You're right."

We chill out in silence for a while—well, as silent as it can get with Livi munching popcorn in my ear—before I say, "So now that Adam isn't around, are you going to tell me your story about the foreign guy?"

"No way. I'm saving that story for when I have your *full* attention, not your Matt-confused brain."

I chuckle, then shove the tissue up my nose again at the dribbles that threaten to escape. "Well, I'm looking forward to a non-Matt-confused conversation about your foreign romance sometime in the near future."

I SPEND SUNDAY AND MONDAY IN BED, SNIVELLING, shaking, dosing myself with all the flu medication I can find in the bathroom cabinet, and tossing the 'Matt or no Matt' question around my head. By the time Tuesday arrives, I'm dreading it for more than one reason. One, I hate New Year's Eve because I'm always pressured into going to some great big social event I feel one hundred and fifty percent awkward at. Two, I've decided what to do about Matt—and I'm pretty sure it's going to land me in the middle of another massive argument before I get to finally say goodbye. I know Matt, and he is not the type to go down without a fight.

Now that my body's functioning normally again and recognises that we're still in the middle of a hellishly hot summer, I stuff all my germ-covered winter pyjamas into the wash basket and pull on some shorts and a tank top. I rush through my breakfast, then struggle to keep it down. I'm terrified of the conversation I have to have with Matt, and it's messing with my stomach. The sooner I talk to him, the sooner I'll feel better. And it has to happen before tonight so I don't have to be dragged to a New Year's Eve party as awful as last year's.

I climb into my oven of a car and wind the window down. "Okay, I can do this," I tell myself. "I can do this." I reverse out of the driveway and hit the button on my remote to close the gate. After making sure it closes all the way, I head off down the road. Part of me hopes that Matt won't be at home—I didn't tell him I was coming—but the rest of me just wants to get this over with.

As I reach the corner, a car turns into our road, and it's only after the driver flashes his lights at me that I realise it's Matt. My heart hammers in my chest as he drives past me, and my car jerks as it stalls. "Fabulous," I mutter under my breath as I turn the key in the ignition. I do a U-turn and follow Matt back towards my house. Great. Looks like this break-up is gonna happen in our driveway.

I open the gate and drive back in. Matt parks in the road, but instead of walking through the gate, he waits beside his car for me. Are we supposed to be going somewhere? Did we make plans that I've forgotten about?

"Hey," I call out as I walk towards him. He doesn't respond, which is a little weird. He's staring at the ground, and as I reach him, he looks up. The sight of his red eyes shocks me.

Wait a freaking second. Does he know I'm about to break up with him? Is that why he's been crying?

"Um, what's wrong?" I ask tentatively.

He reaches out and takes my hand. He sniffs, then says, "Grandpa died last night."

It's a shock to everyone, because it's not like he was sick or anything, but he was old and frail, and I guess it was his time to go. Someone suggests that he was weaker than we all knew, and perhaps he was just hanging on for that birthday and family reunion celebration so he could see all the people he loved one last time. He went quietly in his sleep, and everyone keeps reminding everyone else how fortunate he was that he didn't have to suffer through a long and painful end. But I can't help thinking how traumatising it must have been for Nan to wake up and find him like that in the morning.

The memorial service happens a week later at a church about half an hour from the farm. It's full of laughter and tears and happy stories about the life Grandpa lived. My cheeks are wet along with almost everyone else's. Afterwards, everyone drives back to the farm, and the family—which I'm told I'm part of today—gathers around the bench beside the lake where Nan and Grandpa used to sit on warm evenings. Nan takes the urn and scatters the ashes around the bench and into the water.

I sit with Matt for the rest of the afternoon. Matt, who is

quieter today than I've ever seen him before. He puts his arm around my shoulders several times and tells me how glad he is to have me. How glad he is that he doesn't have to go through this alone. How glad he is that I'm always there for him.

I spend the whole of Wednesday lying on the couch with my laptop perched on top of me. Mom's back at work this week, and Dad's closed up in his study doing something incredibly boring like lesson planning since he'll be spending most of next week at teacher development workshops, and the week after that, school starts. I've got a month left before university classes begin, and the thought of that looming date circled on the calendar hanging in the kitchen makes me feel ill. It's the main reason I've got my laptop set up on top of me and about a thousand browser windows open: I'm researching my options.

I always figured I'd just carry on with my BSc, and somewhere along the line I'd become wildly excited about chemistry and atoms and the structure of amino acids and everything else that makes the world work at its tiniest level. As if my parents' love for this stuff might somehow seep into me as time went by. But the truth is, I hate it now, and I'm probably going to hate it more the longer I continue with it. So even though I'm nowhere near the point where I can say, 'Hey, Mom and Dad, I made a mistake. I'm never going to be a scientist. I just want to make up stories for the rest of my life. I'm sorry for wasting your money. Can I start again?', I'm at least looking into what I *might* be able to do if I'm ever brave enough to tell them something like that.

The movie playing in the background ends, and Sophie flicks to another channel. I click on a link to read about the English courses offered by my university. Ugh, why are they all so boring? Why can't I get a degree by simply writing stories all day long for three years? I click on another link that takes me to a page listing a whole lot of short story competitions I can enter throughout the coming year. Hmm, I wonder if I could make a living by doing nothing else but entering writing competitions? No, that doesn't exactly sound feasible. I'd have to be the best—every single time. And I doubt all the prizes would be large enough to live off. Still, competitions are probably something I should try out, just to see if I'm any good. I can't exactly trust Aiden's opinion after he was caught sneaking my notebook out of my desk. He probably would have said anything to get himself out of trouble at that point.

After a little more Googling, I come across a popular site called *The Hippy Writer's Guide to the Galaxy*. The Hippy Writer, whose real name appears to be Felicity, hosts a monthly writing competition called *Write It or Bite It*. In the first week of the month, people can send in the first three pages of a story. Felicity randomly selects twelve entries, posts all the first pages on her site without the writers' names attached, and readers vote for their favourite. At the end of the second week, the bottom half of the entrants 'bite it,' and the top half of the entrants get to 'write it' by having the second page of their stories added to their entry. After the third week, the bottom three entries get cut, and the final three entries go through to the fourth week with the third page added onto their stories. After the fourth week of voting, a winner is announced.

Cool. I can do that.

I check the date. Dammit, it's the 8th today. But it's the first *full* week of January, so maybe the Hippy Writer is still accepting entries.

I open a new document, chew on my lip for a few minutes, then start writing. This story is going to be *good*. It's going to be *epic*. It's going to knock the socks off every other entry.

On the other end of the couch, Sophie groans and changes the channel again. "Why are chick flicks so *pathetic*?" she moans. "There's always some helpless woman who doesn't know what's missing in her life until some hot guy shows up and basically makes her feel like her life is worthless without him. He gets all macho if another guy shows any interest in the woman, which is apparently attractive instead of being, you know, creepy, and the woman falls all over him thinking how lucky she is that he picked her." Sophie throws the remote onto the couch and stands up. "Ugh. Puke."

"Good point," I murmur as Sophie heads for the kitchen. I press the return key a few times in my document, then type, 'Note: Make sure heroine is strong, confident, and kickass. No helpless, pathetic women.' I scroll back up to my opening paragraph, then freeze with my hands over the keyboard. A light comes on in my brain, blinding me with sudden clarity.

That's me, I realise. *That helpless, pathetic woman is ME.* At school, I was a nobody—and then I became Matt's Girlfriend. When we're at a large gathering of his extended family, I'm Matt's Girlfriend. At varsity, I'm Matt's Girlfriend. I don't know who I am without him! I'm still that swooning girl who can't believe how lucky she is that Mr Popularity picked her. That swooning girl who can't do anything without his approval. I'm not strong or confident or kickass. I'm the definition of a doormat. And if Matt has his way, I always will be.

Just like that, my mind is made up: Matt and I are over.

I WAKE UP ON THURSDAY MORNING EVEN MORE CERTAIN of my decision. I wait for the sick feeling while I'm eating my breakfast, and it's definitely there, hiding somewhere beneath the muesli in my stomach, but something else is beating it down.

Excitement. I'm going to be free!

I park outside Matt's parents' house and press the button next to the gate. It opens a moment later without anyone speaking through the intercom to find out who's outside. Matt already knows it's me. I sent him a message this time so I'd be certain he's home.

He greets me at the front door with a quick kiss, whispers, "I'll be done in a minute," into my ear, then raises his cell phone to his ear to continue a conversation that obviously started before I got here.

I hang my car keys on a hook by the door, wander

through to the kitchen, and sit down at the table. I assume no one else is here, since Matt's parents are back at work and Malcolm doesn't live here anymore. My left knee bounces up and down as I try to stamp my nervousness down so hard I won't be able to feel it anymore. *It's just Matt. This is just a conversation. You're just … ending a two-year relationship with your possessive and controlling boyfriend.*

DON'T. FREAK. OUT.

I breathe in deeply and stare at the fridge. A neat arrangement of family photographs is stuck below a rectangular chalkboard Matt's mom writes reminders on.

Dentist 12 Feb 15:30

Q20

Hannah's sister-in-law in Westville

Below the last note is a phone number, and, like the crazy stalker I am, I whip out my phone and snap a picture of it. Because that's where Aiden's staying, and who knows if I might want to call him before he leaves tomorrow. The only contact we've had since we yelled at each other outside uShaka Marine World was a glance at Grandpa's memorial, so it might be nice to have an actual chat. Apologise, maybe admit that he was right, and say goodbye. I don't expect anything more than that, of course, but it would be nice if we could at least part as—

"Sorry, babe." Matt strides into the kitchen and opens the fridge. "Some people can just talk and talk and talk. You want something to drink?"

"Uh, no thanks."

He helps himself to a bright blue sports drink before

perching on the edge of the table beside me. "So I thought we could go to Gateway and watch that new Tom Cruise movie. I've been waiting forever for it, and it's finally here."

"Actually—" I swallow "—I need to talk to you." I stand up and put a little distance between us. "I don't think ... you and I are working."

His forehead scrunches up. "What do you mean?"

"I mean ..." *Just say it, just say it, just say it.* "I'm breaking up with you."

He stares at me for several moments, and I can see the words aren't making sense to him. They're not the kind of words that have any place inside his perfectly controlled world. He takes a swig of his blue drink, then starts laughing. "Come on, Sarah. Who put this silly idea in your head? Was it Adam and Livi? I know they never liked me that much."

Stand firm. Be brave. "Can you please take me seriously for a change? I mean what I'm saying, Matt. This isn't just a 'silly idea' I came up with while hanging out with my friends."

"You mean what you're saying," he repeats.

"Yes."

He slowly screws the cap back onto his drink. "You're breaking up with me."

"Yes."

"*You* are breaking up with *me*?"

"Yes!" How many times do I have to say this before he'll get it?

A muscle in his jaw twitches. "I can't believe you'd do

this to me just after Grandpa died."

"Oh, don't even try that," I say. "This has nothing to do with Grandpa. This is about you and me and the fact that we are *not good together anymore*. I'm not sure if we ever were."

"Oh, I see." Matt nods. "I get it. This is about Aiden, isn't it?"

"No, it's—"

"Some other guy shows an interest in you, and suddenly I'm not good enough for you anymore."

"No, this is *not* about Aiden. This is about—"

"Seriously, Sarah? You really want to leave *me* to go chasing after someone you can never have?"

Despite the fact that this doesn't have anything to do with Aiden, I raise my chin and say, "Who says I can't have him?"

Matt's hand clenches around the plastic bottle as his mouth twists into a mean smile. "Are you really so stupid, Sarah? Do you honestly not know?"

That look. I know that look. It's the look Matt gets when he's about to deliver a crushing blow. And even though I know he's about to break me with words, I whisper my question anyway. "Know what?"

That twisted grin twists a little further. "He's engaged."

Just like that, I'm transported back to that night. The night before I left to visit Julia. My suitcase is almost packed, I'm in the bathroom decanting shampoo and conditioner into little bottles, and Matt is chilling in my bedroom. I fill my clear plastic toiletry bag with all the right sized bottles, then zip it up and take it back to my room. My large suitcase and my carry-on suitcase are sitting side by side on the floor with their lids open. My excitement mounts each time I look at them.

This is really happening!

I add my mini toiletries to the smaller suitcase as Matt says, "What's this?" He's lying on my bed examining my laptop screen. "'Start your novel in a week,'" he reads out, then looks over at me. "Why are you looking up creative writing courses?"

Butterflies flit nervously around my stomach. I haven't shared my crazy dream with *anyone* yet, but I'm so excited about it, I have to say something. I take a deep breath and twist my hands together. "Well, you know how I write a lot in my spare time. And I was thinking I want to do more with that. Like actually … write a whole novel. I think I could do that. So I was looking up courses."

"But this is some academy in the UK," Matt says with a frown.

"Well, yeah, I know, but—"

"And you happen to be studying in South Africa."

"Yes, but …" I close my eyes and groan. "You know I'm not actually enjoying the science stuff. I love writing stories, so—"

"Sarah, you can't just give up after one year." Matt pushes himself up so he's sitting. "You just need to change your attitude towards your degree, and then you'll start enjoying it.

"Well ..." I hate arguing with him, but he needs to know how I really feel. "I'm not so sure about that. Stories are what I love. And I know that course is in the UK, and I haven't worked out anything about money or study visas or anything, but there are others. All over the world. And lots of them are distance learning ones. So I could be anywhere. So I was thinking, I could do kind of like a gap year thing. Do some travelling and writing, and some working too, of course, and maybe by the end of the year I'll have finished a book. And maybe it'll be good enough to be published. I could be a real author!"

"Sarah." Matt stands up and puts his hand on my arm. "I don't think that's a good idea. I mean, listen to yourself. *Maybe* you'll finish a book by the end of the year? *Maybe* it'll be good enough to be published? What kind of plan is that?"

"Well ..."

"You and I already have a plan, remember? We're at the same university, we've each got our degrees picked out, we work hard, and we're both going to be successful in our chosen areas."

"But ... maybe that's ... your plan," I say quietly. "Not mine."

Matt's eyebrows shoot up. "Excuse me? I hope you're not suggesting that I forced you into anything, because you were the one who decided to follow me."

Yeah, after you suggested it would be a good idea. I'm not brave enough to say that out loud, though. I feel like this conversation got away from me somehow. It wasn't supposed to go like this when I finally told someone that I might have figured out what I want to do with my life.

"I just think it's a major risk to take when you don't even know if you're any good. It's not like you ever let anyone read this stuff you write." He walks to the shelf with all my notebooks. My most recent one is already packed at the bottom of my carry-on suitcase, but all the others are lined up on the shelf my family and friends have always known not to touch. "In fact, why don't we settle this right now." Matt slides a notebook from my collection. "I'll tell you if it's worth the risk."

"Hey! No!" I try to take it from him, but he holds it out of my reach. "Put that back, Matt, it's—"

"Why? Are you hiding something from me?"

"No, of course not."

"Then why don't you want me reading it?" He stands on my bed so I have even less hope of reaching the notebook. I try to think of how to explain that my writing is *mine*. It's private. It isn't ready for anyone else's eyes. But he'll never understand, and he's already reading it anyway, so what's the point? I bite my lip and cross my arms. I pace to the desk and back.

After a minute or so that feels more like an eternity, Matt jumps down from the bed and snaps the notebook shut. He hesitates, then delivers the words he knows will crush me. The words that will put me back in my place. "I'm sorry,

Sarah. You should stick with science." He gives me the kind of smile people give when they feel sorry for someone. And I almost believe him. I almost believe that he does feel sorry for me. But there's something twisted about that smile. Something that isn't right.

My broken heart swells up with anger, and I'm suddenly braver than I've felt in a long time. "That is a *lie*. You're just saying that because you don't want me to go off on my own adventure without you. I could be famous one day, and you'd be left in the background, and that is the *last* place you—"

"Famous? Really?" Matt laughs loudly. "For that to happen, you'd have to actually be *good*. And this?" He waves the notebook in front of my face. "This is *trash*. This is *never* going to be published."

"Shut up!" I shout. "You don't have a *freaking clue* what's good and what isn't. You don't read. You don't know *anything* about—"

He throws the book at me, and even though I raise my arm, the sharp corner hits my chin. "Don't you *dare* speak to me like that!" He leans over me and pauses there, his eyes trained on my face. Probably waiting to make sure I don't dare say another word. "This discussion is over," he says. "Have a nice holiday."

And then he's gone, leaving me shaking in my own bedroom, wondering what the hell just happened and whether my family heard any of it over the movie they're watching in the lounge. I go to bed soon after that, burying my head beneath the duvet so no one can hear me crying. And then, because I'm obviously in complete denial, I keep my head buried for the entirety of my holiday overseas, doing my best to put the whole thing out of my mind.

I blink, bringing myself back to the present. Back to that mean, twisted smile and those words hanging between us.

He's engaged.

"That's right," Matt continues, a triumphant gleam in his eyes. "Didn't you know? Her name is Kelly. Lovely girl."

Matt thinks he's won. He thinks he's broken me. But he doesn't know that this was never about Aiden. It's all about him. So I push those words aside to think about later and focus instead on the guy standing in front of me.

"Stop it," I say, quietly but firmly. "Stop trying to hurt me. Stop trying to control me. This relationship is over, and I am *not* yours to be controlled."

"YES YOU ARE!" Matt flings his bottle across the room. It strikes the sink and blue liquid explodes from the top, splattering the wall and the clean dishes standing in the drying rack. "This is *not* how we end. *You* do not break up with *me.*"

"News flash!" I yell at him. "It's already happened!" And before he can say or do anything else, I'm out of the room. I grab my keys from the hook by the front door, press the remote on whoever's keys are still hanging there, and run out of the house. My hands are shaking so badly I almost drop my keys on the sidewalk, but I manage to get into the car and pull onto the road without stalling.

Tears drip down my cheeks as I drive back home, which is really confusing, because what I'm feeling above all else is exhilaration. It must be the shock of the whole thing. The shock of finally standing up to Matt. The shock of reliving that fight and the book being thrown in my face—which, now that I think about it, he never even apologised for! What a *jerk*!

A jerk who'll never be able to influence you again, a quiet voice reminds me. A snotty-sounding laugh escapes my lips, and it sounds so ridiculous it makes me laugh even harder. And now I'm crying and laughing and sniffing and I *really* hope no one pulls up next to me when I get to a traffic light, because I probably look like I need to be escorted to a mental health institution pronto.

It's only after I've been sitting in my car in my parents' driveway for about five minutes forcing myself to do some slow breathing that I remember what Matt said about Aiden.

He's engaged.

My mind rejected the words the instant I heard them, but the longer I think about it, the more sense it makes. Aiden told me he used to be close to his sister, but not anymore. When Elize mentioned Emily's wedding, Aiden and Emily exchanged a glance that certainly meant something. Then Aiden missed a call from someone—a female someone—and his mother wanted him to return the call, but Emily didn't. So all of that could mean that Aiden is engaged to a girl who, for whatever reason, his sister doesn't like.

But if he's engaged to someone, why did he kiss me at the airport?

Maybe he's having second thoughts about his wedding. Maybe that's why he didn't answer when she called.

But why didn't he say anything to me about her? How dare he get upset with me for not mentioning my boyfriend when he neglected to mention his *fiancée*? He's *engaged*, for crying in a bucket—or, in this case, a car. How did he manage not to bring that up even *once* during our many hours of talking? And how dare he challenge me about not being brave when he didn't even have the guts to mention his upcoming *wedding*?

Oh, man, I am *so* over boys right now.

I pull my phone out of my pocket and find the picture with Aiden's aunt's phone number. I memorise the numbers, then furiously tap them into my phone's keyboard and press 'Call.' It takes about three rings before I realise I'm about to talk to a stranger on the phone—one of my Big Fears in Life. But I just managed to break up with my boyfriend who turned out to have scary anger issues, so I can DO THIS.

A woman answers the phone. "Hello?"

I clear my throat. "Um, hi, may I please speak to Aiden?"

"Uh, yes. Who is this?"

"Sarah."

"Hold on a minute, Sarah."

I hear muffled noises in the background, then Aiden's voice. "Hey, Sarah?"

"Hi."

"I was just trying to figure out how I should go about getting your phone number. I've been wanting to—"

"Are you engaged?"

Pause. "What?"

"Engaged. You know? Here comes the bride and all that? Or, in this case, here comes Kelly."

Another pause. "You know about Kelly?"

"Yes."

"Well then you should also know that—"

"Why didn't you tell me?" I ask, proud of myself for managing to keep the wobble out of my voice, despite the fact that I'm almost in tears again. "If you had a right to get mad about me not mentioning Matt, then don't I have a right to get mad about you not mentioning her?"

"It isn't like that, Sarah. Kelly and I—"

"No. I don't believe you let me explain why I didn't mention Matt to you on the plane, so you don't need to do any explaining either."

"Sarah—"

"You're leaving tomorrow, right?"

"Uh, yeah. I—"

"Well have a nice flight." And I end the call.

"So, uh, I'm going to my flat in Pietermaritzburg tomorrow," I announce at dinner on Thursday evening.

"Mmm." Dad catches a pea that fell from his fork and adds it to his mouth. "Okay."

Mom looks up and frowns, though. "But varsity doesn't start for another four weeks."

"Oh yes." Dad adds his frown to Mom's. "What do you need to go to Pietermaritzburg for?"

"Really? Is it so impossible to imagine that after living there for a year I might have formed some kind of life there? You know, friends and stuff? And do you still need to interrogate me about my plans when I'm a year out of school now?"

Mom pulls her head back slightly and Dad forgets he's holding a forkful of food in front of his mouth. Even Sophie looks a little shocked.

"Okay, sorry. Um, if you must know …" I take a deep breath. "Matt and I broke up."

"What?" says Sophie.

"Oh, honey, I'm so sorry." Mom looks appropriately devastated as she reaches across the table to clutch my hand. "What happened? When? Are you okay?"

"It's fine. I'm fine. Really. It's something I should have done a while ago."

"*You* broke up with *him*?" Sophie looks surprised.

"Yes." I try not to get upset as her words remind me of what Matt shouted in my face earlier. "Is there something wrong with that?"

"No, it's just a little unexpected."

I suppose it is.

"Is this something that's … permanent?" Mom asks carefully. "Or just, like, a big fight?"

"It's permanent," I say firmly. "He's possessive and controlling and I don't want him in my life."

Mom looks horrified. She turns to Dad and says, "How come we didn't notice that?"

I poke the piece of chicken on my plate with my fork. "He's good at hiding it," I say quietly. "I mean, it took me all this time to figure out, didn't it?"

"Well, you are kind of a pushover," Sophie mutters at her plate.

"Excuse me? How dare you—"

"What? I just mean that—"

"Stop it," Mom says over both of us.

"Did he hurt you?" Dad asks, his frown deepening. "You

said he's possessive and controlling. Was that just verbally, or—"

"I'm fine, Dad. I promise. Can we move on now please? Because I'd really like to. That's why I want to go to 'Maritzburg. I just want some time out."

Mom nods. "Of course. That sounds like a good idea. You have some friends there, don't you?"

I nod. There are some people I could probably call friends. People Matt and I have hung out with over the past year. But no one I'd consider confiding in like I would with Livi or Adam or Julia. Mom doesn't need to know that, though. She also doesn't need to know that I plan to spend all my time alone in my flat working on the project I haven't told a single person about. The project I'm finally going to see through from beginning to end.

I love my Pietermaritzburg flat. It's in the back garden of a house that one of Mom's old school friends lives in with her five hundred—excuse me, I mean seven—cats. It's quiet, surrounded by a pretty garden, and I'm only ever visited by one cat at a time.

I stock my kitchenette with zoo biscuits, biltong from the Ashburton Butchery—voted best biltong in KZN in 2012—chocolate covered raisins, fresh lemons to add to the large amounts of iced water I plan to consume, and a small amount of real food. When Saturday morning arrives, along with the sun and the birds and the sweet scent of all the flowers filling the garden, I open up the document with those three pages I entered for the 'Write It or Bite It' competition, and I'm ready to go.

It takes me ten days. Ten whole days of slogging away at my tired old beast of a laptop—with regular backups in case the beast suddenly dies—but at the end of it, I've finally achieved something I've wanted to do for years.

I've written a book.

A first draft, of course. It's nowhere near polished. But it's a book! An entire, freaking novel! I grab the cat who happens to be visiting at the moment and do a happy dance in the middle of my tiny living area with the unfortunate animal. When it starts to look like it might take a swipe at my face, I drop it onto the couch, turn up the music on my laptop—which, fortunately, is connected to a set of speakers of far greater quality than those inside it—and dance from one side of my open-plan flat to the other. The cat blinks at me and I wiggle my butt in its face. Most embarrassing dance ever, but the bushes growing over the walls of this property are too thick for any neighbours to see through. I checked when I first moved in here.

I plop onto the couch with a happy sigh. That was fun, but I need to share my joy with more than a cat. I want to tell someone—and not just any someone. I want to tell Aiden. He's the one who said I should finish a story. He's the one who believed it could be a bestseller one day.

I check my phone to see what time it is. Monday, 9:46 pm. England is two hours behind us, so that puts it at 7:46

pm wherever Aiden is. Hmm. There's a whole list of things he could be doing right now. Finishing dinner, working, watching TV, hanging out with Kelly. Crap, maybe he *lives* with Kelly. I'm not the sort of person to move in with someone before I'm married to them, but Aiden might be. Not that it should matter, though, because I'm not planning to send him a message declaring my undying love for him. I just want to share my achievement. That's what friends do, right? They tell each other about the big things they've done.

I still don't have an email address or phone number for him, so Facebook it is. I go to the app on my phone and search for Aiden's page. I hit the 'Message' button, then stare at the last words we exchanged: He apologised for getting upset that I hadn't told him about Matt and asked if I still wanted to be friends. I said yes.

I try to figure out what to say now. Going straight into 'Hey, guess what? I wrote a book!' doesn't seem like the best way to start after our last interaction where I told him to have a nice flight and hung up on him. So … an apology is probably a good place to start.

Sarah: I'm sorry I was so rude to you on the phone. I'm sorry I hung up without giving you a chance to say anything. If you still want to tell me whatever it was you were going to tell me, please do.

And then I wait. I tap my finger on the side of the phone, watch other posts come up on the news feed, and resist the temptation to write another message to Aiden.

Perhaps I should have a shower. I've been glued to my computer all day—approaching the end of the story seemed to make my fingers fly faster and faster over the keys—and with the amount of sweat this hellish summer is making me produce, a shower is definitely in order. I leave my phone on the edge of the basin so I'll hear if a message comes through, but it doesn't make a single ping, ding, or trill while I'm showering.

Afterwards, I climb into bed with one of my old favourite books that's been living in this flat for most of the past year: Harry Potter Number Three. After making sure that my phone is on the bedside table, I open to a random page and settle back against the pillows. I don't know how much time passes—I tend to become oblivious to the world around me when I'm reading—but Harry has just found out that his broom has been smashed to pieces by the Whomping Willow when my phone makes a chirp beside me. Clearly I'm not oblivious enough to miss that. I grab the phone and open the message.

Aiden: I didn't think I'd hear from you again.

A small "Eeeee" escapes my throat, and I have to force myself to calm down before I reply. But then I can't think of what to type. I mean, he hasn't explained what he was going to say on the phone, so does that mean I've lost my chance? Will I never know? Maybe he's angry with me. He didn't use any smileys, so maybe he's about to tell me to get lost and not contact him again. I'm saved from having to figure out what his message and lack of smileys mean when he sends another message.

Aiden: So you want to know what I would have said to your 'Are you engaged?' question?

Sarah: Yes.

Aiden: No.

No? What does that mean? Is it 'No, I'm not going to tell you' or 'No, I'm not engaged'?

Aiden: Kelly and I were engaged, but we broke it off about eight months ago. I'm not involved with anyone.

Seriously? That's it? I throw my head back and groan, partly because I hit my head on the wall and partly because I'm so frustrated with myself. Why didn't I just let him say that over the phone? Why didn't he shout it out before I hung up?

Aiden: Who told you anyway?

Sarah: Matt.

Aiden: Cousin Matt and I communicate a maximum of about once a year, usually to leave a quick 'happy birthday' message on Facebook, so it's not surprising he missed the part where Kelly and I broke up.

Sarah: Or maybe he was trying to hurt me.

Aiden: Why would he do that?

Sarah: I was breaking up with him at the time.

There's a minute or two of silence after that, then the next message pops up.

Aiden: I hope you didn't do that purely because *I* said you didn't want to be with him.

Sarah: No. I did it because *I* didn't want to be with him.

Sarah: Remember you asked why I was crying on the plane?

Aiden: Yes.

Sarah: Matt and I had a major fight the night before I left for England. He was violent and scary. The things he said to me ... they were meant to hurt me. They were meant to break my spirit. And then he didn't contact me at all the whole time I was away, and I spent the whole time pretending it had never happened. But I had to start thinking about it once I was headed home. I had to start wondering if we were even together anymore. That's why I didn't tell you I had a boyfriend. I wasn't entirely sure if I did. And I know I shouldn't have left it up to him to decide. I should have made the decision for myself the moment he walked out of my house that night. But ... I didn't know what I wanted, and it was easier just to leave the decision up to him.

Aiden: Choosing to end a relationship can be tough, even if you know that person isn't good for you.

Sarah: It was terrifying, but remarkably liberating :-)

Aiden: :-)

I stare at that little smiley with a great big dorky grin on my face. And then, because I clearly *am* a dork, I make a comment about the weather.

Sarah: Is it still super cold there?

Aiden: Uh ... I've been colder.

Sarah: Did you have any panic attacks on the flight home?

Aiden: No more height- or flying-induced panic attacks.

Sarah: Good :-)

Sarah: Um ... Can I ask you a question?

Aiden: I'm all ears. Or, in this case, eyes.

Sarah: Who was the girl you and your mom and sister were arguing about when we arrived at uShaka? The call you missed?

It takes so long for him to reply that I think he may have gone offline. But then an essay-long message pops up.

Aiden: That was Kelly. Lately she's been sending me texts and leaving messages saying she thinks we should give our relationship another chance. I told her I'm not interested, but she obviously doesn't believe me. The reason Mum and Emily were arguing about it is that Emily never liked Kelly. Em and I used to be really close, but I changed after I met Kelly, and not exactly for the better. Our relationship was kind of like … an emotional bungee jump. We thought we were madly in love, but in the end, we just weren't healthy for each other. Em saw that, but Mum didn't because she lives further away and Kelly and I didn't visit her that often. And we were obviously on our best behaviour when we did. So Mum always thought Kelly was lovely, and she never really understood why we broke up. I guess she thinks that if I have a chance to work things out with Kelly I should. Fortunately, I know better.

Aiden: Wow, I think that's the longest message I've ever written on Facebook! My thumbs thank me for using my computer instead of my phone.

I read through the message as puzzle pieces I'd forgotten about add themselves to my picture of Aiden's life. I remember him sitting at the Häagen-Dazs table frowning at a message on his phone—which was probably from Kelly. I remember his reaction when Elize talked about Emily's wedding being the first wedding in their family—because Aiden's would have been first if he and Kelly hadn't broken up. I remember him telling me happily ever afters are a myth—because he thought he was getting his happily ever after, but it didn't happen in the end.

Sarah: I'm sorry. That all sounds quite hectic.

Aiden: Don't be sorry. I'm certainly not! If we hadn't broken up, we'd be married by now, and we'd both be living in some kind of nightmare. Not to mention that I must have been smoking something to think I was ready to be married at age 23.

Sarah: Were you?

Aiden: What?

Sarah: Smoking something.

Aiden: Ha ha! No :-)

Sarah: Okay. Good :-)

Aiden: Can I ask you a question now?

Sarah: Of course.

Aiden: Why did you wait so long before contacting me? I've been hoping every day to see a message from you. I wanted you to know the truth.

My heart grows wings and flies right out of my chest. He's been *hoping* to hear from me! He actually *wanted* me to contact him! But instead of typing a hundred smileys followed by a hundred exclamation marks, I manage to keep my cool.

Sarah: Why didn't you just send a message instead of waiting for me?

Aiden: It didn't seem like you wanted to know the answer to your question. I thought I'd wait until you did.

Sarah: Well, I picked now because I wanted to tell you something. And I couldn't just launch into it without first apologising for that phone call. And that meant admitting that I should have let you talk instead of hanging up on you.

Aiden: So the thing you wanted to tell me is …

Sarah: I wrote a book! An entire book. Not just an outline or a few scenes. A. WHOLE. BOOK.

I don't know why he makes me wait so long for his response, because when it finally comes, it isn't exactly a long one.

Aiden: WOOOOOOOOOOHOOO!

Sarah: :-)

Aiden: I believe I deserve to be named in the dedication. Or at least the acknowledgements. After all, I was the one who snooped through your desk, read one of your notebooks, and told you how brilliant your stories are.

Sarah: I named a character after you.

Aiden: Seriously?

Sarah: He dies halfway through the book.

Aiden: WHAT? :-(

Sarah: A very heroic death.

Aiden: I guess that's not so bad then.

Sarah: :-)

Aiden: Except that now I KNOW WHAT HAPPENS!

Sarah: Oops ... Spoiler alert.

Aiden: It's too late for that.

Sarah: I know ;-)

Aiden: I'm so sorry, I actually have to go now. But this conversation definitely isn't over.

My soaring heart falls back to earth, and I contemplate typing a whole row of sad faces. That would probably come across as way too needy, though, so I manage to restrain myself.

Aiden: One more question, though.

Sarah: Yes?

Aiden: What's your book about? (Judging from the number of notebooks in your bottom drawer, I'm guessing you had about 753 ideas to pick from.)

Sarah: 754 actually.

Aiden: Right, sorry. So ... it's about ...

Sarah: You'll have to read it to find out ;-)

TUESDAY 21 JAN

Aiden: Are you back in Durban now?

Sarah: Yes. Ten days alone in my PMB flat got a little lonely.

Aiden: It was certainly productive, though.

Sarah: That's an understatement!

Aiden: Your parents must be very impressed.

Sarah: I haven't told them yet. They thought I was just hanging out with friends for the past week.

Aiden: WHAT?

Aiden: You? 'Hanging out'? You don't seem the type ;-)

Sarah: Dumbass. I am completely capable of HANGING OUT with people I feel COMFORTABLE with.

Aiden: You know I'm just joking, right?

Sarah: :P <— this is me sticking my tongue out at you.

Aiden: \~>|<~/ <— this is a bunch of symbols representing me pulling a weird face at you.

Aiden: Seriously, though, you should tell your parents. Writing a book is just as awesome as being an award-winning photographer or a popular artist. (BTW, I looked at both Julia's and Sophie's pages on FB and yes, they are both incredibly talented. But I have no doubt that one day your FB fan page will have even more fans than theirs.)

Sarah: :-) <— beaming face

Sarah: Anyway, I WILL tell my parents. I'm just … still thinking about things.

Aiden: Okay.

Sarah: Okay :-)

Aiden: So … I did a little research into this biltong stuff you seem so attached to.

Sarah: Oh yeah?

Aiden: Yes. Did you know it technically means 'buttock tongue'?

I let out a snort-laugh I'm highly grateful Aiden isn't around to hear. I lean back in my desk chair and shake my head at the computer screen.

Sarah: It does not.

Aiden: Want to make a bet on that?

Sarah: Uh ... no?

I quickly open another window and navigate to my online dictionary of choice. I type in the word 'biltong' and wait for the result. Hmm. Well, what do you know. Aiden's actually right. When I get back to the Facebook page, his next message is already there.

Aiden: You're looking it up, aren't you.

Sarah: I just did.

Aiden: So now you know I'm right :D <— this is my 'I told you so' face.

Sarah: What a weird meaning for a snack so awesome.

Aiden: As weird as eating it.

Sarah: Maybe, but I'm still gonna eat it!

Aiden: I should probably tell you that I tried some today.

Sarah: What?! Where did you find it? I was craving biltong the whole time I was in England.

Aiden: A South African specialist store.

Sarah: Cool. So what did you think of it?

Aiden: ...

Sarah: Well?

Aiden: I was having a salt craving. So ... it was pretty good.

Sarah: TOLD YOU SO!!

WEDNESDAY 22 JAN

Aiden: I used to try and talk to God.

Whoa. Okay, that came out of nowhere. Especially from someone who made it pretty clear he doesn't believe in God. I press the 'Mute' button on the TV remote and lie down across the couch. Dad's in his study doing school stuff, Mom's on her bed reading through the corrections she received on a paper she recently submitted to a journal—which I'm certain is the most boring type of reading EVER—and Sophie's in her room, probably drawing something on her computer and enjoying having no homework yet. Bottom line: There's no one here to ask why I'm now finding my phone more absorbing than I've ever found it before.

Sarah: And?

Aiden: He never answered me.

Sarah: Is that why you decided he isn't real?

Aiden: Yes.

Sarah: Were you waiting for an audible voice?

Aiden: I think I was.

Sarah: Hmm. I think God talks more in other ways. Like signs. Coincidences (which, if they really are from God, aren't coincidences at all).

Aiden: Why?

Sarah: I don't know. Maybe to make sure people are really listening. Or, you know, 'listening.'

Aiden: Do you want to know what I was thinking after you pulled me to the edge of that cliff and made me look out at those mountains?

Sarah: Yes.

Aiden: I'd never looked down at the world from such a height before. I'd never seen so much of its beauty in one moment. I remembered what you said on the plane about life not always being about things you can see or hear or touch. Sometimes it's more than that. And I stood there and thought … Could all of this really have happened by chance? Could it really exist without meaning anything?

Sarah: That's quite deep from someone who thinks the idea of a creator is ludicrous.

Aiden: I have my moments ;-)

Sarah: :-)

Aiden: And then we huddled under a tree in the rain, and you started telling me you didn't believe in coincidences. That things don't just happen by chance, and that everything means something. And I wondered if the fact that you were talking about the very thing I'd just been contemplating was a coincidence in itself, or if that, too, meant something. And now you're telling me you think God speaks to people through coincidences, which aren't coincidences at all. So I'm thinking … that means …

Sarah: Maybe He is talking to you after all.

Aiden: Maybe ...

THURSDAY 23 JAN

Aiden: We never had our secret rendezvous on Christmas eve :-(

Sarah: I know. I was going to give you a dictionary. And inside the Christmas card I was going to write, 'Look up the word intriguing.'

Aiden: I was going to give you a T-shirt with the words ZOO BISCUIT FREAK on it.

Sarah: I want that!

Aiden: It was an imaginary Christmas present. It can never exist in real life.

Sarah: Nonsense. Of course it can. And it should. You should make one.

Aiden: Maybe I should. I'll become a T-shirt-making scientist.

Sarah: As opposed to ... ?

Aiden: A biltong-making scientist?

Sarah: No, silly. I mean what kind of scientist are you now, in real life?

Aiden: Oh. I'm a trying-to-figure-out-what-to-do-with-my-life scientist.

Sarah: Hey, me too!

Aiden: Officially, though, I pretend to know a lot about genetics.

Sarah: Pretend?

Aiden: After five years of study, I feel like I should know more than I do.

Sarah: I think I might be pretending too if I go back to the same degree this year ... No way do I want to end up at year five thinking, 'I don't have a clue why I'm still doing this.'

Aiden: Fortunately, it's not that bad for me. I actually enjoy what I do. I just don't know where it's taking me next. I was hoping my solitary journey around Europe might help me figure it out, but ...

Sarah: No light bulb moment?

Aiden: Not yet. What about you?

Sarah: Well ...

Aiden: ??

Sarah: I have an idea. But I'm afraid my parents will say no.

Aiden: Only one way to find out.

Sarah: I know, I know.

Aiden: Can they really stop you from doing what you want to do, though?

Sarah: Well, I don't exactly want to do a Julia and skip the country! It would be nice to have their support in whatever I choose to do. (Also, I barely have any savings, so I kinda need their financial support too!)

Aiden: So what is this idea?

Sarah: If they say yes, I'll tell you all about it ;-)

Aiden: Oh, the suspense!

Sarah: You won't have to wait long. Mom's going to be home in about

Sarah: Strike that. She just got home. Wish me luck!

21

I RUSH INTO THE KITCHEN JUST AS MOM DUMPS HER BAG ON the table. Dad walks through from his study—he got home about twenty minutes ago—and gives her a quick kiss before opening the fridge.

"Hi, Mom. Dad. Um, can I talk to you?" I stand in the kitchen doorway twisting my hands together.

Mom looks up from where she just plugged her cell phone in to charge. "Yes, of course." She presses a few buttons on her phone, then leaves it on the counter and turns to me. "What's going on?"

"Maybe, uh, we should all sit down."

Mom and Dad exchange a glance, then each take a seat at the table. I slide into a chair opposite them.

"This sounds serious," Dad says.

"It is." They took my choice of tertiary education *very* seriously after Julia abandoned her medical school plans and ran away from home. They wanted to make sure I was choosing what *I* wanted to do and not what *they* wanted me to do so that I wouldn't end up wasting time on the wrong degree. Which is exactly what I've ended up doing.

"Well, what it is?" Mom asks, worry lines creasing her forehead.

"Uh … well …"

Mom's hand grips the edge of the table. "You're not pregnant, are you?"

"WHAT?"

"Well, it's not entirely impossible—"

"Oh my GOODNESS, Mom!"

"We raised her better than that," Dad says to Mom, rubbing her arm.

"Thank you, Dad."

"Well, I'm sorry, but you said Matt was very controlling, so it's possible he could have pressured you into—"

"No. Mom. Stop." Flames engulf my face. "This has nothing to do with Matt."

"Oh. That's good." A relieved smile crosses her face.

Dad clears his throat. "So this is about …"

"I wrote a book."

"A book?" Mom says, as if I'm speaking an alien language.

"Yes. A novel. That's what I was doing in Pietermaritzburg. I wasn't visiting friends. I was writing."

"Well, that's quite impressive," Dad says.

"You did always enjoy writing in those many notebooks of yours," Mom adds.

"And, so, this is also about the fact that I hate what I'm currently studying."

"Oh." Mom looks less impressed now.

"Yeah, um … so the truth is that I really didn't know what to pick when I left school. So I went for a BSc because I'd always kind of enjoyed Physics and Chem and Bio, and you guys are both in the science field and love what you do, so I figured … I'd end up loving it too. But I don't. It's getting worse with each month that passes. I sit in class wishing I was doing something else—and then my brain starts making up stories to, you know, pass the time or entertain myself or whatever, and then I realised that that's what I should be doing. Stories. Books. Writing."

"So … you want to switch to a BA?" Mom asks. "Major in English?"

"Well, no. I don't want to go back to university."

All eyebrows in the room except mine shoot up. I knew this was going to be the difficult part. Mom and Dad have always made it pretty clear they want us to get a degree or qualification of some kind after school so that we'll have, as they always say, 'something to fall back on.' Julia, of course, rejected that route and proved she could make a living doing what she loves. I need Mom and Dad to see that I can do the same thing.

"I don't mean that I'll just hang out at home for years writing books and living off my parents," I say. "I have a plan. There are courses, you see." I lift the pages I printed earlier from where they've been hiding on my lap. "They're not, like, whole degrees, but that's because they'll teach me exactly what I want to know without all the extra stuff a degree would have that I'm not interested in." I spread the pages out on the table. "There are lots of different creative writing courses, many of them distance learning. So, um, I thought for this next year I could live at home and do some courses to improve my writing, and I'll work and write at the same time. Obviously not a major job, since I don't have a qualification, but, like, at a bookstore or a library—" surrounded by books all day! "—and when I've polished my writing, I'll look into all the various publication routes, and … at the end of it all I'll be a published author."

Mom and Dad look a little alarmed at my outburst. I don't generally say so many words at one time. After a shared glance, Mom looks back at me. "Well, we obviously don't want to stop you from doing what you really love—"

"Of course not," Dad chimes in.

"—but you understand that this is a risky choice, don't you? There's no guarantee that you'll be able to make enough to support yourself as a writer. You never know if a book will publish or not, and if it does, you can't predict whether it'll be successful."

"Well, there's no guarantee that I'll find a job when I've finished my BSc either. In fact, I probably won't. I'll have to continue into Honours and Masters, and even then, who knows if I'd get a job or not?"

Mom considers that. "Yes, I suppose that's also true. Not many people get decent jobs with only a BSc these days."

"There's always teaching," Dad says.

"Come on, Dad." I give him an are-you-serious look. "You know there's no way I'm ever going to be a teacher. I'll be too scared of my students to be able to teach them anything."

Dad chuckles. "We all have to start somewhere."

"No. Teaching is one thing I know for certain I'll never do."

"Okay, okay." Dad holds his hands up in surrender, then looks at Mom. "We already have one daughter who took a leap and followed her dream. We can't exactly stop Sarah from doing the same thing."

Mom looks at me. "As long as you know the risks and you're determined to work as hard as you can, then of course we'll support you in this."

"Really?" I clasp my hands together as excitement explodes in my chest. "Thank you, thank you!"

"Well, of course," Mom says with a laugh. "Did you really think we'd force you to continue studying something you hate?"

I get up and run around the table to hug her. "Thank you," I repeat.

"The only other thing I have to say," she adds, "is thank goodness you figured this out after first year instead waiting until the end of your degree."

I wrap my arms around Dad next to make sure he doesn't feel left out. "I never would have lasted that long."

I run back into my room and land in my desk chair with such force I almost knock it over. I open the lid of my laptop and wait for the screen to blink on so I can tell Aiden what just happened. Then I'll have to tell Livi and Adam. And Julia, of course. She'll be so excited for me.

Motion in my doorway makes me look up, and I see Sophie leaning into my room. "Congratulations," she says with a smile.

I swivel my chair so I'm facing her. "You were listening?"

She nods. "You didn't really expect me *not* to listen after I walked past the kitchen and heard Mom ask if you're pregnant, did you?"

I start laughing. "I have *no* idea where she came up with that one."

Sophie shakes her head. "So I guess you're going to be living at home full-time this year."

"Yes. Why? Were you enjoying being an only child during the week?"

"Are you kidding? I hated it! Mom and Dad pay way too much attention to me when I'm the only one around."

"Well, don't worry, they'll be paying attention to me now. They'll want to make sure I'm not just taking an easy year off."

"Good." We share a smile. "Anyway,' she continues, "it's probably a weird coincidence that this happened at the same time, but I got an email from artSPACE just now. I've been on their mailing list since I went to that exhibition. But this event isn't about *art* art. They're hosting a live poetry and short story reading at the end of the month, and—" she twirls a strand of hair around her finger "—I thought you might be interested."

"In going?"

"In taking part. I forwarded you the email. Anyway, I gotta get back to my desk. First homework for the year." She mimes puking, then disappears from my doorway, leaving me with nerves suddenly jumping up and down in my stomach. Me? Take part in a short story reading? Standing in front of a bunch of strangers and reading my work out loud? Sophie is insane. There's no way I can do that.

But I open up my email anyway and stare at her message sitting right at the top. **artSPACE Live Poetry and Short Story Reading**. *Just read it*, I tell myself. *Reading it doesn't mean you've agreed to anything yet.* I click on the email and go through the details. The event is happening next Thursday night. People are invited to come along and listen, and, since the programme isn't yet full, anyone interested in taking part is asked to contact the event organiser by Monday.

I don't have to do this. No one's forcing me to. I could ignore the email and relax next Thursday night like I do every other night. No need to panic and stress myself out. But there's a tiny yet persistent voice at the back of my mind that keeps whispering something. *Fly. Be brave. Take a chance.*

I think of Aiden facing his fear head-on and stepping up to the edge of the mountain. I think of him daring me to talk to those two strangers at the restaurant. I think of how I failed. But … I can't believe I'm actually thinking these words … if he can conquer his fear, so can I. I click the 'Contact Sandy using this form' link. I fill in all the requested information and hit 'Send' at the bottom of the form before I can come to my senses and back out of this. Then I return to Facebook and type another message to Aiden.

Sarah: I'm going to try and fly. Will you catch me if I fall?

I'M STANDING FROZEN IN FRONT OF MY MIRROR WITH MY
printed-out story in my hands when my phone interrupts
my terrifying visions of tomorrow night. I peer over my
shoulder at my desk and see a Facebook message from
Aiden on my phone's screen.

> **Aiden:** So ... I could probably introduce any topic
> beneath the sun for us to discuss this evening and you'd
> bring it right back to how you're panicking about
> tomorrow night.

I grab the phone and throw myself onto my bed, which
turns out to be a horrible idea, because hitting the mattress
with my stomach makes me feel even closer to throwing up.
I take some slow, deep breaths before replying.

Sarah: Who says I'm panicking?

Aiden: You're not? That's great!

Sarah: I. Am. Freaking. INSANE. I am BEYOND panicking. What on earth possessed me to think I could actually do this? I'm freezing up in front of MYSELF for goodness sake. What am I going to do in front of a whole room full of people?

Aiden: Um … imagine them naked?

Sarah: That is the stupidest thing ever. I don't know who came up with that advice for banishing public-speaking phobia, but whoever it was clearly did NOT know what it's like to experience REAL fear when a whole crowd's attention is on you. I tried that during orals at school, and it did NOT work.

Aiden: But you survived then, so you'll survive now.

Sarah: Maybe I won't. Maybe I'll die of fear.

Aiden: Kind of a pathetic way to die, don't you think? If you're going to go toes up due simply to fear, at least wait until you're face-to-face with a lion or a knife-wielding psychopath or a time travelling T. rex.

Sarah: Thanks. You're really helping.

Aiden: Am I? It's hard to tell whether you're being sarcastic. :-/ <— confused face.

Sarah: You're helping so much that all my fears have magically transformed into happy little sunbirds that are flitting away into a rosy sunset.

Aiden: Sarcasm. Got it.

Sarah: I'm sorry! I've tried practising out loud, and it goes fine if all I think about is telling myself a story. But as soon as I imagine doing it in front of a crowd, I can't seem to get the words out.

Aiden: Focus on the people you know. Your parents or Sophie or anyone else you've invited. Look ONLY at them. Then you won't feel like you're talking to strangers.

Sarah: Are you nuts? I haven't TOLD anyone I'm doing this. It's bad enough embarrassing myself in front of people I don't know. Now you want me to do it in front of people I DO know?

Aiden: You won't be embarrassing yourself.

Sarah: You don't know that!

Aiden: Take Sophie with you. Seriously. Tell her to sit in the front row and ONLY look at her. That's my last piece of advice.

Sarah: I wish I could take you.

Whoa, what? I am being *way* too honest for my own good right now. It's too late, though, because as advanced as cell phones are these days, they don't yet seem to include a 'Bring that message back right now' button. So now it's sitting there at the bottom of our conversation, and Aiden is taking his sweet time replying.

No reply.

No reply.

WHY HASN'T HE REPLIED YET? I've probably scared him away forever. He's probably figuring out a way to quickly end this conversation and—

Aiden: I wish I could be there.

Oh. My. Hat! It seems I may have been right about my fears transforming into happy little sunbirds, because all I can feel right now is a ridiculous sort of gleeful giddiness.

Sarah: You do?

Aiden: Of course. The only place I've wanted to be since I first met you is at your side.

Aaand the sunbirds are doing crazy happy flapping all around my insides. It's utterly insane, because Aiden and I might as well be a gazillion miles apart, and who knows when we'll see each other again, but I can't help the fact that he's the first person I think of when I wake up and the last person I say goodnight to before I fall asleep, and the person I want to hear from every moment throughout the day, and I think I might be kinda crazy about him, AND HE LIKES ME BACK!

> **Aiden:** Sorry. My brain lost control of my fingers for a moment. I really wasn't planning on making you feel uncomfortable when you have something way more important to focus on tonight. Just forget that last message!

WHAT? Forget that last message? As if I could EVER erase those words from my brain. What could possibly be more important than this moment? If he thinks I'd rather be panicking about tomorrow night, he obviously has no clue how I feel about him. Which seems somewhat impossible considering we've fit about ten years worth of conversations into the ten days since I finished writing that book. Does he think I communicate this much with every guy I know?

I reread his message, then type my response.

> **Sarah:** Why would I feel uncomfortable?

> **Aiden:** (Feeling super relieved we're not having this awkward conversation face-to-face.) Well, you know, it's always uncomfortable when a guy admits that he might sort of … have feelings for a girl when he knows she doesn't feel the same way.

My body attempts so many reactions to Aiden's words at once that I think I short-circuit the emotion section of my brain, which leads to the calm response I type next instead of the Aaaaah!!??:-D!!??Eeeee:-)))) that might have come out otherwise.

Sarah: How do you know I don't feel the same way?

Aiden: (:-/ Confused face again.) Um, well, you never replied to my letter, so that was the only logical conclusion.

Sarah: What letter?

Aiden: The letter at the end of the book.

Sarah: What book?

Aiden: The pink book. The book I almost left the airport with. The book you said you finished reading.

"What the heck?" I mutter. I jump up and scan my bookshelf for the romance novel I borrowed from Julia and never finished reading after I arrived back in Durban. It was silly, frivolous stuff, after all, and I had far better books waiting on my to-read pile beside my bed. I snatch the book from between *Harry Potter and the Deathly Hallows* and *I Am Number Four* and flip through the pages near the end. There's the last page of the story, then the acknowledgements, then—WHAT IS THAT?

On the blank space after the second page of acknowledgements, before the page about the author, hastily written words have been penned in black ink. HE WROTE IN THE BOOK! If he were anyone else, I'd probably want to smack him for violating the pages of a novel, but these are Aiden's words, and if I didn't want to read them so badly, I'd probably be kissing the page.

Sarah,

I stood in front of you, and there were a thousand things I wanted to say, but I couldn't figure out how to say any of them without COMPLETELY shocking you. How do you tell a person you only just met that you think they might be the one to show you happily ever afters aren't a myth after all?

So I walked away. And then I started to panic: The universe (or God, as you'd probably say) gave me a second chance by putting you next to me, and I might be throwing it away by not being brave enough to tell you how I feel. And then I realised I STILL HAVE YOUR BOOK! And now I'm writing in it, and of all the words swirling about my head and my heart, the only thing I have time to write is … I want to see you again. I don't want to say goodbye. I don't want this to be it. And maybe you think I'm crazy, and you're glad you never have to speak to me again, so that's why it's all up to you now. If this comes out as insane to you, then you can ignore it. You need never see me again. But if not—if you feel the same way I do—tell me. Answer me. I want to see you again.

You said your life is messed up at the moment. Well so is mine. Isn't everyone's? No one is perfect. And if we keep waiting for that moment when everything in our lives is neatly in place, we may end up missing what's standing in front of us right now.

Aiden

ARHarrison@me.com

The sunbirds have burst into flame. My whole body is hot and my hands are shaking and I'm not sure I'm even breathing anymore and I can't believe this letter has been here the WHOLE TIME! Ever since Aiden ran back into the airport, put it into my hands, and kissed me. Of course I felt the same way! I still do!

I grab my phone from the bed, and it slips from my sweaty fingers. I deposit my butt on the floor and try again, holding it in both hands this time. Looks like I missed several messages while I was searching for and reading the letter.

Aiden: ???

Aiden: I swear I can hear crickets chirping.

Aiden: ????????

Aiden: Okay, seriously. You have to say something now.

My fingers fumble over the screen as I try to type a reply as quickly as I can.

Sarah: I never finished reading the book. I didn't know you wrote a letter.

Aiden: Well ... this is awkward.

Sarah: But if I had, this is how I would have responded: I want to see you again. I don't want to say goodbye either. I don't want this to be it. I don't think you're crazy or insane, and I want to be the one to show you that happily ever afters DO exist.

There's a pause that lasts about a million seconds. Then—

Aiden: I want to kiss you.

I fall back on the carpet before my ridiculous giddiness can knock me out.

Aiden: I want to be right next to you.

Sarah: WHY ARE YOU SO FAR AWAY?!

Aiden: It won't be forever.

Sarah: Really?

Aiden: We'll figure something out.

Sarah: I'll never be able to fall asleep tonight.

Aiden: Me neither. I'll be wishing you were next to me.

Sarah: :-)

Aiden: :-)

23

AIDEN MADE ME PUT MY PHONE AWAY AT 11 PM MY TIME SO I could get a decent sleep and be fresh for today, but I was so excited it took me at least two hours to fall asleep. Then I woke up early and couldn't get back to sleep because I kept thinking about him. At least it kept me from thinking about the reading tonight, which, now that it's only two hours away, is beginning to take over my thoughts again.

After a cold shower to try and combat the effects of the heat and humidity—unsuccessful, as always—I get back to my bedroom and see something sitting on my pillow. I pad across the carpet to get a closer look. It's a blue zoo biscuit with a dolphin on it, sitting on top of a piece of paper with the words 'I know you'll be amazing tonight!' printed on it.

A wide grin is stamped on my face as I pick up the biscuit and the note. I make sure my towel is wrapped securely around me before I walk to Sophie's room. She's sitting cross-legged on her bed doing her homework. At least, I assume it's homework. "Do you know anything about this?" I ask, displaying the biscuit for her to see. She looks up, plastering an innocent expression on her face.

"A biscuit? Why would I know anything about a biscuit?"

That grin is back on my face. "You're a terrible liar," I tell her.

"I know."

"Will you be ready to leave in forty minutes?"

"Yip."

"And you told Mom and Dad I'm taking you there to see an art exhibition?"

"Yes. There actually is an art exhibition happening there, so it wasn't even a lie."

"Which is obviously why they believed you," I say with a wink.

I hurry back to my room to get ready and try to think about the zoo biscuit and Aiden instead of the audience I'll soon be standing in front of.

Tonight's event, titled *A Twist in the Tale*, is taking place in the main gallery of the artSPACE. The gallery lights are slightly dimmed, and fairy lights are strung around the room. Ivy twists around the pillars. Paintings interpreting the theme are displayed on the walls, and the poems and short stories being read tonight will all incorporate something relating to the *Twist in the Tale* theme. Chairs are set out between the pillars, but most people are walking around admiring the art.

I wander around the room with Sophie, trying to pay attention to what she's telling me about the artworks rather than throwing up on them. First there's a painting by an artist who seems to have taken the theme quite literally. It's of a cat with a curly pink tale that looks like it belongs to a pig. Next is something a little more intriguing. All that's visible in the frame of the picture is a man's foot hovering above a glass running shoe. A woman's hands are holding the shoe, and it looks like the man's foot is about to try the shoe on. So this is ... Cinderella in reverse. Interesting.

But SO not interesting enough to distract me from my panic. I pull Sophie into a corner and grip her shoulders tightly. "I can't do this. We need to leave. I'll send a message to the organiser and say I got sick or something. It's not exactly a lie, because I'm pretty sure I'm about to be sick all over—"

"You *can* do this, Sarah, and you're going to be amazing, just like the Zoo Biscuit said."

"His name is Aiden," I remind her. We went over this several times in the car.

"Well, he'll always be Zoo Biscuit to me."

"I *can't* do this!" I almost shriek at her.

"Hey, calm down." She looks around to see if anyone noticed my temporary loss of sanity. "Remember that you're only going to be talking to me. And I've already heard your story at home, so I probably won't even be listening, which means you'll really only be talking to yourself. Easy, right?"

"Wrong."

"Let's just stay until it's your turn in the programme. Then if you *really* can't get up there, we'll just run out of here."

We find two seats in the front row that haven't yet been claimed, and I attempt some deep breathing while everyone else, who seems at least five hundred times calmer than I am, examines the art before slowly finding themselves a place to sit. Sophie shows me the programme for the evening, and I find my name second from the end. WHY? Now I have to sit through every other item before I'm allowed to run away. I'm never going to last that long.

A lady walks to the front of the room. Once the audience is quiet, she thanks everyone for coming and talks briefly about something I try hard to focus on but fail to hear. Then she introduces the first person on the programme, a poet. As he stands and walks to the front, Sophie—my sweet little sister—reaches for my hand. Perhaps it's less about her being sweet and comforting, though, and more about her planning to yank me back into my seat if I attempt a getaway before it's my turn.

It's painful listening to everyone who goes before me, mainly because they're so darn good. Some of them are practically performing their poetry, never mind simply reading it. Their words are punctuated with dramatic pauses, hand gesticulations, and scary facial expressions.

No way am I doing something like that.

We move closer and closer to my name, and I feel more and more like passing out. When the lady introduces me, Sophie squeezes my hand. "You can do this," she whispers. "Your story rocks. *Nobody* is gonna see that ending coming."

I stand up, and instead of running out of here, my shaky legs carry me to the front. I stare at the papers in my hands. They're a little crumpled by now, and the edges are covered in damp marks from my sweating fingers, but the words are all still there. My words. My story. And Sophie's right. It *does* rock. I look up at her, refusing to let my eyes wander to the rest of the audience. She gives me an encouraging smile and a thumbs up.

Spread your wings and fly, that little voice says.

I look back down at the page. I clear my throat, swallow, and begin.

My first instinct is to race through the words as fast as I can, but, with extreme difficulty, I force myself to go slowly and keep breathing. I was taught at school that it's good to look up at the audience every few moments when reading something, so I glance at Sophie every time I remember to breathe. Other than that, I focus on the story itself. I remember how excited I was when I came up with that twist at the end. I remember Sophie's gasp when I first read it to her. I remember the poets and their dramatic pauses, and I force myself to hesitate a moment before delivering that final sentence.

Then I lower my pages. I look up and allow myself to see the roomful of people for the first time. Every person's attention is on me, their hands still and their eyes wide.

Silence.

"Thank you," I murmur, then hurry back to my seat as the room erupts with applause. It sounds like the same kind of applause they gave to everyone else, but Sophie grips my arm and squeals in my ear.

"That was *amazing*. They all *loved* it."

I'm floating on a cloud of relief and exhilaration, and I don't hear a single word the last person says. I tune back in just as the organiser lady thanks everyone once again and invites us all to enjoy the snacks, drinks and artwork.

I stand up and throw my arms around Sophie. "Thank you for coming with me. Thank you for making me do it."

She laughs. "Well, I was under strict instructions not to let you run away," she says into my ear.

"Instructions? Instructions from ..." My words trail off as my gaze falls on someone behind her. Someone familiar. Someone tall with an adorable grin and a dimple in his left cheek. Someone who can't *possibly* be standing there for real. "What ... how did he ..." I pull away from Sophie, who turns to see what I'm looking at.

"Ah. That must be Zoo Biscuit."

My brain can't quite process the fact that Aiden is standing in this room—in this *country*!—but my legs know what to do. I run and fling my arms around him. He stumbles backwards into a section of wall between two artworks, but he's laughing in my ear, so I don't think he minds that I just about attacked him.

"You rocked that story," he says to me.

"Who cares about the story?" I pull back slightly, but

keep my arms looped around his neck. He's HERE and he's HOLDING ME and I'm floating WAY beyond cloud nine right now. More like cloud gazillion and nine. "What are you doing here?"

"You didn't really think I'd miss this, did you?"

"But ... you live so far away. And you hate flying."

His blue-green eyes sparkle as he smiles. "I never went home."

"What?" I shake my head in confusion. "But you said you were leaving."

He nods. "I did say that. And I did leave. But not for home. I've been in Joburg staying with a friend of mine. We studied together until about a year ago when he moved here. After Kelly and I ended things, I told him I was looking for a new direction with my studies. When he heard I was visiting South Africa, he suggested I stay a bit longer and check out the options here."

"The options here? The options HERE? In South Africa?" Does that mean what I think it means?

"Yeah, well, not everyone wants to leave this country. Some of us think it has a lot going for it. Like the warm climate and the friendly people and—" he raises his hands to gently cup my face "—this one particular amazing girl."

I open my mouth, but no words come out.

"I'm going to kiss you now," he says. "Any objections?"

I shake my head and pull his face closer to mine. Our lips meet, and then I'm shooting beyond the clouds and into the galaxies. I don't think my feet will ever touch the ground again. His hands are in my hair and I'm pressing him against the wall and I can't get enough of his lips and his mouth and OH, MAN, this kiss should NOT be happening in public. His lips move across my cheek and down to my neck.

"There are people here," I remind him breathlessly.

"Oh, yeah." He pauses, then kisses my nose. "Including your parents."

"WHAT?" I jump away from him, looking around. Did my parents just see me lip-locking with Aiden? SO embarrassing. I don't care how old I am, I do not need my parents seeing stuff like that.

"Relax." Aiden pulls me closer once more. "They said they'd hang out by the snacks and give me a chance to talk to you."

"You told them about tonight?"

He nods. "I hope you're not mad at me. I figured that if I were them, I'd hate to miss this. They hid in the back row with me. We didn't want to freak you out before you went up."

I take his hands and wrap them around my waist. I stand on tiptoe to kiss his nose. "I'm not mad at you."

"Do you want to go talk to them?"

I shake my head. "I want you to myself for just a little bit longer. If you're okay with that."

"I'm more than okay with that." He presses his lips against mine for a moment, then says, "We can start working on our happily ever after, which, if I've understood all the fairy tales correctly, is supposed to begin the moment after our first kiss."

"In that case," I say, "our happily ever after started after you kissed me at the airport."

"True." A thoughtful expression crosses his face. "So what does our happily ever after look like then?"

I loop my arms around his neck. "It looks like … secret letters in the backs of books, and hikes in the rain, and challenging each other to face our fears."

"And texting late at night and first thing in the morning."

"And misunderstandings and arguments and make-up kisses."

"And dancing." He twirls me around and pulls me back.

"Especially crazy happy dancing," I add with a giggle.

"And the way you smell like the ocean." He kisses my neck.

"And your accent that makes me want to swoon."

"And stories and zoo biscuits and biltong."

"And feeling safe." I rest my head against his shoulder as he wraps his arms around me. "The right kind of safe."

"The right kind of safe," he murmurs. "Even when you have no idea where life will take you next."

"Even then."

"This is a happily ever after I can do."

I smile against his T-shirt and whisper, "Me too."

epilogue

From: Felicity, the Hippy Writer
<felicity@hippywritergalaxyguide.com>
Sent: Sat 1 Feb, 8:42 am
To: Sarah Henley <s.henley@gmail.com>
Subject: 'Write it or Bite It' January Competition

Dear Sarah

Congratulations! Your story took **first place** in the January 'Write It or Bite It' competition! You've won a spot on our Hall of Fame page along with an interview feature on the main page of The Hippy Writer's Guide to the Galaxy (see attached questions). Many voters commented on how they wished they could read beyond the first three pages of your entry. We urge you to continue with this story and hope to one day see it as a completed work on bookstore shelves.

Thank you for entering 'Write it or Bite it'!

Kind regards,
Felicity, the Hippy Writer

VISIT

WWW.TROUBLESERIES.COM

FOR BONUS MATERIAL BASED ON
THE TROUBLE WITH FLYING

AND DON'T MISS OUT ON THE REST OF
THE TROUBLE SERIES!

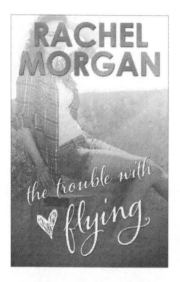

RACHEL MORGAN

the trouble with ♥ *flying*

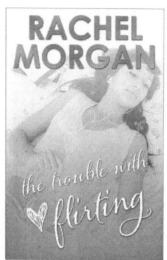

RACHEL MORGAN

the trouble with ♥ *flirting*

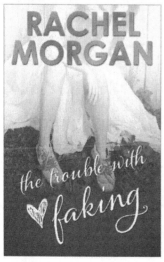

RACHEL MORGAN

the trouble with ♥ *faking*

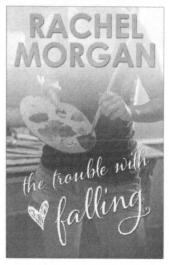

RACHEL MORGAN

the trouble with ♥ *falling*

ACKNOWLEDGEMENTS

Thank you, God, for speaking to me through coincidences, for allowing me to grow up in one of the most beautiful countries in the world, and for showing me that you exist not only in the magnificence of creation, but in the most intricate workings of the universe.

Thank you, Katie, for being the very first reader of *The Trouble with Flying*, and for loving Sarah's story.

Thank you, Mariska and Nicola, for saving the reading world from my abysmal Afrikaans skills by translating Elize and Simone's words into Afrikaans that makes sense.

And thank you, Kyle, for being my happily ever after, my right kind of safe, and for letting me fly.

© Gavin van Haght

Rachel Morgan spent a good deal of her childhood living in a fantasy land of her own making, crafting endless stories of make-believe and occasionally writing some of them down. After completing a degree in genetics and discovering she still wasn't grown-up enough for a 'real' job, she decided to return to those story worlds still spinning around her imagination. These days she spends much of her time immersed in fantasy land once more, writing fiction for young adults and those young at heart.

Rachel lives in Cape Town with her husband and three miniature dachshunds. She is the author of the bestselling Creepy Hollow series and the sweet contemporary romance Trouble series.

www.rachel-morgan.com

Made in the USA
San Bernardino, CA
11 February 2020